*A
Harlequin
Romance*

1465

DAMSEL IN GREEN

by

BETTY NEELS

HARLEQUIN   **BOOKS**
TORONTO   ●   WINNIPEG

First published in 1970 by Mills & Boon Limited,
17 - 19 Foley Street, London, England.

SBN 373-01465-1

© Betty Neels 1970

Harlequin Canadian edition published February, 1971
Harlequin U.S. edition published May, 1971

*All the characters in this book have no existence outside the
imagination of the Author, and have no relation whatsoever to
anyone bearing the same name or names. They are not even
distantly inspired by any individual known or unknown to the
Author, and all the incidents are pure invention.*

The Harlequin trade mark, consisting of the word
HARLEQUIN and the portrayal of a Harlequin, is registered
in the United States Patent Office and in the Canada Trade
Marks Office.

Printed in Canada

CHAPTER 1

THE church clock across the street chimed the half hour, and Miss Georgina Rodman, already walking down the corridor leading to Casualty, put on a sudden desperate turn of speed. There was a chance—a faint one—that she might arrive on duty before Staff Nurse Gregg; if she didn't, it would mean the third time late on duty in a week, and Gregg would probably report her to Sister. It would be of no use making excuses, for Gregg never needed to make excuses for herself, and couldn't understand why anyone else should either. Nurse Rodman wasted precious breath on a sigh as she ran, for her excuses were good ones—on Monday it had been the ward maid falling downstairs with that large pan of porridge; the porridge hadn't been hot, but extremely sticky; thinking about it, Georgina couldn't see how she could have ignored the girl's cries for help. She had been late on Thursday too, when she had met a rather down-trodden old lady who had been told to attend for a barium meal at seven-thirty in the morning, and didn't know where to go. It had only taken a very short time to walk with her to X-Ray—just long enough for Staff Nurse to remark triumphantly:

"Late again, Nurse! You should know better—how can you hope to set a good example to the juniors? And you waiting for the results of your Finals!"

Her tone had implied that Georgina need not expect good news. And now it was Saturday, and she was late again, for she had stopped to ask Payne the head porter how his wife was feeling; the poor soul had been ill for weeks, and Payne had been looking sad. She pulled up outside Cas. swing doors and drew a breath. It was a pity that life didn't allow you time to dawdle a little on the way. She opened the doors, to find Staff Nurse Gregg waiting for her—doing the dispensary of course, because that was her particular job in the mornings;

but she had dragged the basket into the centre of the room so that she wouldn't miss Georgina.

She looked pained. "Late again, Nurse Rodman—the third time this week! I shall have to report you to Sister—there might have been a terrific emergency on."

Georgina said, "Yes, Staff" because it was expected of her, and went to twiddle the knobs of the sterilizers in an expert way and count the packets of dressings and instruments C.S.D. had just sent down. The two junior nurses had already prepared the cubicles for the day. She slipped quietly in and out of them, making sure that everything was just so. They were two nice girls, but Staff's bullying ways made them careless. There was an empty oxygen cylinder in the second cubicle and no dressings at all in the fourth. The fifth contained a tired-looking boy, a bare, grubby foot on the stool before him, clutching his shoe and sock.

"Trodden on a rusty nail?" asked Georgina in a friendly voice. She was already busy cleaning it up.

"How did you know?" asked the boy.

"We get a great many—it's a common accident. It'll be fine in a day or two—you won't need to stop work, but I'll have to give you an injection." She gave him a nice wide smile and went to find Staff. She wasn't a trained nurse yet—she couldn't give A.T.S. without getting permission. Gregg gave it with the air of conferring a great honour.

"Why didn't you leave the boy? It's nothing urgent," she wanted to know.

"He's on night work, it would be a shame to keep him from his bed."

Staff frowned. "You'll never make a good nurse," she grumbled, "you're so impetuous."

Georgina gave the injection, wondering why she was impetuous. Surely it was plain common sense to clear the cubicles of the minor cases as quickly as possible, otherwise there would be such a bottleneck later on in the morning. She wrote up the boy's card, filled in the day book, tidied up neatly and went into the last cubicle. Both nurses were in it, as she had guessed they would be. They grinned cheerfully at her, and the

6

youngest and prettiest said. "Oh, George, isn't she in a foul mood?"

Georgina grinned back. "It'll be worse if you don't get a porter to change the oxygen in Two . . . and there aren't any dressings in Four." There was a hurried movement for the door and she added, "I've seen to the dressings, but it'll look better if you report the oxygen."

They stopped at the door. "George," said the nurse who had forgotten the dressings, "we wish you were staff."

"That's nice of you both, but I expect I've failed my State, you know."

She turned to the tiny mirror on the wall to straighten her cap. She had fine, silky hair, and the cap needed a great many pins to keep it at a dignified angle. It was pretty hair, too, light brown and long, and she screwed it up into a severe plaited knob at the back because it was quick to do and stayed tidy that way. She looked at herself in the little square of glass while she re-planted some pins. The face that looked back at her was a good-looking one; not pretty—the nose was a trifle too large and the chin a thought too square, but the brown eyes were large and clear, like a child's; their lashes long and curling and thick. The mouth was large too, a generous mouth with corners that turned up and smiled readily. Her complexion was a child's too, which flushed easily when her feelings were aroused—a fact which annoyed her excessively. She was neither tall nor short and a little on the plump side and looked considerably younger than her twenty-three years. She gave the bib of her apron a tweak and made for the door—it was time to dish the bowls.

She had just put the last two in their appointed places when Sister appeared in the doorway. She was a small, very neat woman in her thirties with a quiet voice which she never raised, however trying the circumstances, and a keen sense of humour she kept well damped down under a placid manner. She said, "Good morning, Nurse," in a voice which gave Georgina no clue as to her mood. She returned the greeting and wasn't at all surprised when Sister went on, "Come into the office, will you, Nurse Rodman?"

Georgina put the Cheatle forceps back in their jar and followed Sister across the wide expanse of Casualty to the little office. She shut the door behind her and stood in front of the desk, waiting to be told off.

"Sit down," said Sister surprisingly. She put her hand in her pocket and handed Georgina a letter. "I thought you would like to have this as soon as possible," she said, and smiled. "If you would rather open it alone, I'll go outside."

Georgina turned the envelope over and looked at its back; it told her nothing, so she looked at the front again. "Please don't go, Sister" she said at last. "If I open it quickly it won't be so bad."

This piece of female reasoning was obviously one to which Sister could subscribe, for she nodded and said:

"That's quite true—the quicker the better."

Georgina undid the envelope with fingers which shook a little, and read the letter therein, then she folded it tidily and put it back in its envelope. When she spoke it was in a tone of great surprise.

"I've passed!" she said.

"Well, of course you have, you silly girl," said Sister bracingly. "No one expected you to do otherwise." She smiled kindly, because it wasn't all that time ago that she had felt just the same herself. "You'd better go to Matron, hadn't you, Nurse?"

Georgina got to her feet. "Yes, Sister, of course. Thank you for letting me come in here to read it."

She got to the door and had the handle in her hand when she was astonished to hear Sister say, "Congratulations, George. You deserve it."

Everyone called her George; it was inevitable with a name like hers. The housemen probably didn't know she had another name anyway, and even an occasional consultant had occasionally addressed her so; but no Sister had ever done so before. She flashed a delighted smile across the little room. It was, she realised, a very nice compliment.

She was the last in the queue outside Matron's

8

office—a gratifyingly long one. There was an excited and subdued hum of voices; everyone had passed; no one had let St. Athel's down. They went in one by one, and came out again in turn, looking pleased and slightly unbelieving. When it was at last her turn, Georgina knocked, entered and stood, as she had stood so many times before, in front of Matron's desk, only this time she was bidden to take a chair.

Matron congratulated her with just the right mixture of motherliness, authority and friendliness and then asked :

"Have you any plans, Staff Nurse?"

Georgina gave this careful thought. She hadn't dared to plan—there was some dim idea at the back of her head that she would like to go abroad—but there was Great-Aunt Polly to think of. She said finally, "No, Matron."

"Splendid. I feel sure that when you have had a little more experience we shall be able to offer you a Sister's post."

Georgina so far forgot herself as to goggle. "Me?" she uttered, regardless of grammar. "A Sister? Would I do?" she asked ingenuously.

Matron smiled benevolently. "You will do very well. Think about it—I believe you have a splendid career before you."

Georgina found herself out in the corridor again. There was no one in sight, so she felt free to execute a few skips and jumps to relieve the excitement Matron's words had engendered. Even in these days of the nursing shortage, it was a signal honour to be offered the chance of a Sister's post within half an hour of becoming State Registered. She paused by one of the tall narrow windows overlooking the busy street outside. Matron had said, 'A splendid career'. It occurred to Georgina at that moment that she didn't much care for the idea. At the back of her mind was a nebulous dream of a husband and children—an indistinct group rather like an out-of-focus family portrait hanging on some distant wall; the children indefinable in number and vague in appearance, and the man even more so,

for she had no idea for whom she sought. Certainly she had not found him so far, and even if she did, she would have to wait and see if he felt the same way....
Her train of thought was brought to an abrupt halt by the sound of the ambulance siren, joined within minutes by a second. Her interesting speculations were wiped from her mind as she sped along the corridor in the direction of Cas. There was still no one about, so she did the last few yards at a frank run, with the uneasy thought that nurses never ran except for fire and haemorrhage; well, there was no fire as far as she knew, but there was very probably haemorrhage. Sister was at the outer double doors, already thrown back and fastened. Georgina checked the trolleys; it was vital to have everything in a state of readiness. Minutes, even seconds counted with someone badly injured. The ambulances, very close together, their blue flashers on, turned into the bay before the doors.

"I'll take the first, Staff. Take the second—Staff Nurse Gregg is off until two, so is Jones; but we've got Beamish, and Peck's on at ten." She turned away as the first case was carried in and laid carefully on the first of the trolleys. A man, Georgina saw, before she gave her full attention to the second stretcher—another man, not a very young one either and in bad shape as far as she could see. He looked very blue.

She said, "Good morning, Bert—'Morning, Ginger" to the ambulance men, then, "Wait a second." She opened the flaccid lips and felt around inside them with a gentle finger, then said comfortably, "Let's have these out of the way", and put the false teeth on the pillow. The unconscious face lost its blueness; she turned it to one side and said, "O.K." and they wheeled the trolley into the second of the cubicles. "R.T.A.?" she asked.

Bert nodded. "Lorry and a car—the other two's not too bad, I reckon, but these chaps—they've copped it. T'other went through the windscreen, this chap's had the wheel in his chest."

They were in the cubicle by now, and the two men were already busy easing off the man's boots while Georgina turned on the oxygen and fixed the catheter in one pale, pinched nostril. She regulated its flow very precisely and then started to cut away the man's clothing to reveal the bloodstained shirt beneath. The ambulance men had already slipped an emergency dressing pad beneath it—they drew small hissing breaths of sympathy as her scissors snipped through the last few inches of sodden vest and exposed the patient's chest. Exactly in its centre there was an irregular depressed wound, several inches in diameter, still bleeding freely. Georgina began to swab it gently—it was a wonder that the man was still alive. She had almost completed her task when a man's voice said from behind her:

"Let's have a needle and syringe, George, and get him cross-matched for some blood—he's going to need it. Get some A.T.S. into him too, and let's have the rest of his clothes off and take a look at the damage."

The owner of the voice had come to stand beside her and was already feeling with careful fingers. Georgina, quite undisturbed by the spate of orders, handed him a syringe and needle and started to unscrew the lid of the Path. Lab. bottle. "Hallo, Ned," she said quietly. She liked the young Casualty Officer; he was keen on his work and clever enough at it not to pretend that he knew everything. He said now:

"This one will need I.C.U.—if we can patch him up sufficiently to get him there."

They worked steadily. The ambulance men had gone after an exchange of cheerful goodbyes. There was a subdued hum of talk from the waiting room beyond the cubicles, where the slight injuries—the cut hands; broken collar-bones, minor scalds and burns which filled the benches with an almost monotonous regularity each day were waiting patiently or not, according to the individual. Georgina could hear the clerk taking particulars and answering questions in a calm voice which contrasted oddly with the occasional strident tones of someone who felt particularly hard done by. They had just got the blood transfusion going, not without difficulty, when the Surgical Registrar joined them. Georgina liked him too; he was resourceful and tireless and quiet.

She had often thought that he and Sister were well suited, and had several times suspected that they shared that view themselves. She hoped so. He stood between them now, looking down at the patient. "Intensive Care, Ned, and then theatre—there may be something we can do." He went on, "Congratulations, George. What a way to celebrate!"

She was clearing up the small place with an urgent, methodical speed. Said "Thank you," but had no time to say more, for Ned interrupted:

"George, you've passed—wonderful! We knew you would, but it's nice to see it in writing, isn't it?" He laughed over at her, and she spared a moment to smile back. He really was rather a dear.

She turned away to help the porters lift the patient on to the trolley which would take him to the I.C.U. "I'll go up with him," she murmered. "That blood will need an eye on it."

When she got back, the other patient had been warded too, and Ned was dealing with the other two men who had been in the crash. She started to work methodically through the waiting patients, putting them in the cubicles, cleaning the cuts and grazes, gently swabbing the burns and scalds, easing shoes off sprained ankles, and stockings off old tired legs with varicose veins on the point of bursting, assessing their needs, so that by the time Ned was free once more, he was able to work smoothly down the line of cubicles, with a nurse behind him doing the dressings, while Georgina filled them again as rapidly as they were emptied.

The morning wore on. They snatched their coffee as and when they could get it; indeed, Georgina had barely tasted hers when she was called away to take a toddler to X-Ray; its young, distraught mother insisted on going too, very white-faced and passionately remorseful. She repeated over and over again, "Oh, if only I hadn't left those safety pins on the table!"

Georgina was holding the small boy carefully; they hadn't been able to discover if the pin had been closed when he had swallowed it—a large one would have stuck, but apparently this one had been very small, small enough to go down a long way before it would begin to do any damage.

"Try not to worry," she said kindly. "Children swallow things all day and every day, you know. There's no reason to suppose he won't be as right as rain in a day or two. He'll be quite safe in the children's ward, and you can stay with him if you like."

The young woman cast her a look of gratitude out of all proportion to her words—perhaps it was the kindness in Georgina's voice. When they parted at X-Ray she managed a smile and Georgina found herself promising to go and see how the small boy was doing when she went off duty that evening. She hadn't really time to do so, she reminded herself ruefully, as she sped back to Cas. It was her day off the next day, and she had a train to catch at seven that evening, but the woman had looked so lost....

She was very late for dinner, but the theatre staff were late too, so that there were half a dozen of them sitting at the table. Two of them had taken their exams with Georgina, and, like her, had passed, but unlike her they were leaving to get married just as soon as they could. Listening to their happy chatter, she felt a small shiver of apprehension; supposing Matron's 'splendid career' was to be her lot in life? She pulled herself together with an effort, aware of a discontent quite alien to her nature. She was a very lucky young woman, and Great-Aunt Polly would be delighted. She poured herself another cup of tea from the pot they had persuaded the dining room maid to wheedle from the cook on duty, and entered wholeheartedly into the serious discussion as to whether bridesmaids looked better in full-length dresses or something frankly mini.

Gregg was on duty when she got back, and half an hour later Sister went for her rather tardy half day. Georgina was putting a collar and cuff bandage on a small cyclist who had broken a collar-bone and Ned was washing his hands while she did it. Sister had popped her head round the door as she went and wished them a quiet day, and when she had gone he said in the most casual of voices:

"They'll make a wonderful pair."

"Who?" she frowned an enquiry as she tucked in loose ends.

"Good lord, George, do you go around with your head in a bag? Sister and old Bingham, of course."

Georgina helped the boy on with his coat and tucked the useless sleeve tidily in the pocket, then sent him outside to the clerk's desk before she replied, "They're going to be married, you mean? I knew they were friends." Although now she thought about it, the Registrar did come very often and sometimes unnecessarily to Cas. She took the towel from Ned and dried her own hands, and said gloomily, "I'm glad, they're both dears, but Gregg will be Sister."

He gave her a quick look. "I shouldn't be too sure of that, George."

She had straightened the couch, and now began to refurbish the trolley.

"You know, Ned, this ought to be a marvellous day, and it isn't. I feel at least forty, with nothing left to live for."

He turned at the door, laughing. "You need a husband, my girl. Who shall he be? Tall, dark, rich and handsome; clever of course, and ready to buy you all the tea in China."

She made a face at him. "That'll do splendidly to go on with."

"Good. In the meanwhile, talking of tea, I'm going to get some—there's sure to be a cup going in Men's Surgical. That's where I'll be if I'm needed."

Georgina nodded understandingly. Ned had a roving eye, which had settled, for the time being at least, on the pretty staff nurse on Men's Surgical. She hoped that there wouldn't be anything much in, so that he could get his tea in peace.

He was in and out all the afternoon. A steady trickle of minor injuries kept her busy, for Gregg had established herself at Sister's desk, ostensibly to write up the books, but Georgina's sharp eye had seen *Harpers*

Bazaar and *Vogue,* not quite out of sight. She hoped, with as much temper as her nice nature was capable of, that Gregg would be up to her eyes all the evening, and the whole of the next day too.

She went off duty half an hour late and on the way along the corridor to the Nurses' Home remembered her promise to the mother of the pin-swallowing baby, and had to turn and fly back again and up two flights of worn stone steps to the children's ward. As she suspected, he had been operated upon that afternoon in order to preclude perforation. He was lying in his cot, still drowsy from the anaesthetic, and his mother was sitting with him. Georgina spent several minutes listening to her troubled little voice, nothing in her relaxed manner betraying her impatience to be gone.

She caught the train by the skin of her teeth. Great-Aunt Polly lived in a small village in Essex, some miles from Thaxted. It had been Georgina's home since she had gone to live with Aunt Polly; that had been when she had been a little girl of nine. Her father, a schoolmaster, had died suddenly and unexpectedly from 'flu, and her mother had died a week or two after him, leaving a bewildered little daughter, as frightened as she was unhappy. Great-Aunt Polly had carried her off to live with her in her small timbered cottage, and had been father and mother to her ever since. Georgina sat in the train, looking out of the window at the dreary London suburbs, thinking about the old lady. She would be able to repay her now with a hundred and one small comforts. She frowned at a particularly frowsty row of blackened houses the train was thundering past. She might even save enough to buy a car. . . . She lost herself in a daydream which lasted until the train slowed down at Thaxted. She picked up her case and jumped out, an attractive girl in her well-fitting corduroy coat and high boots. She paused for a moment and drew a deep breath of air, happy to have left London behind her.

The small, rather ramshackle local bus from Thaxted, the last from that town for the day, took her to within a stone's throw of the cottage. The bus was almost empty and she sat just behind the driver, a man who lived in the village and knew her well. They exchanged news and gossiped comfortably until he deposited her within a short distance of her home. She walked the last few yards quite slowly, although she was anxious to be indoors. The cottage stood a little way down a narrow lane leading off the village street. There was an ancient hornbeam on the corner, and on the opposite side the apple trees at the end of her aunt's garden, even on a dark November evening, combined to make a lovely picture in the cold moonlight. She unlatched the little gate and walked, a great deal faster now, up the brick path and beat a tattoo on the Georgian brass door-knocker before opening the door and going in. The passage was brick too, a little worn in places and covered with an Afghan rug, also worn, but still splendid. The back door faced her and each wall held two doors, from one of which a plump elderly woman bustled.

"Miss Georgina! It's nice to see you, that it is. Miss Rodman's had her supper and I've kept yours hot... put that bag down, and go and see her. Did you pass?" She peered at Georgina anxiously and was swept into a violent hug.

"Yes, Moggy, I did. Isn't it wonderful? I'll tell Aunt Polly."

She opened another door and went into the sitting room where her aunt was waiting. She sat, as she always did, in a stiff-backed chair, her almost useless legs on a little Victorian footstool, her sticks on either side of her, so that she need not ask for help if she should want to get up. She hated to ask for help— Georgina had been almost sixteen when Great-Aunt Polly had been stricken with polio, and could still remember very clearly the look on the old lady's face when her doctor had told her that it was not very likely that she would walk again. She belonged to a generation who didn't discuss their ailments; she hadn't discussed them then, but over the following years she had progressed from wheelchair to crutches, and finally, to sticks. Georgina and Mrs. Mogg, who had been with them for as long as she could remember, had watched her struggles and said nothing, knowing that that was what she would wish, but the day Aunt Polly took her first awkward steps with her two sticks Georgina had gone down to the Three Bells in the village, and come back with a bottle of hock under one arm, because she wasn't sure what to buy anyway, but quite obviously the occasion called for celebration. She crossed the little room now and slid on to her knees beside her aunt's chair and hugged her, just as she had hugged Moggy, only with a little less vigour because Aunt Polly was a small dainty person despite her will of iron.

"I've passed," said Georgina, knowing that that was what her aunt wanted to hear.

Aunt Polly smiled. "Yes, dear. I knew you would, of course, but congratulations all the same—I'm very proud of you."

Mrs Mogg had come in with a tray on which was Georgina's supper—steak and kidney pudding and a nice assortment of vegetables and a little baked custard for afters. Georgina got up and took the tray from her, put it on the floor and sat down beside it, and Miss Rodman said:

"Mrs. Mogg, will you get the glasses and the Madeira? We must drink Miss Georgina's health—and you eat up your supper, child, you must be hungry."

Georgina fell to. She had an appetite and enjoyed good food. She had sometimes thought that it would be nice to be taken out to one of the more luxurious restaurants in London and given some of the exotic dishes she had read about, but the only men she went out with, and that not very often, were young doctors with no money and enormous appetites, and she was far too kind to do anything else but agree when they suggested beef-burgers and chips.

Mrs. Mogg came back with the wine, and they sat, the three of them, drinking it from very old, beautiful glasses which she fetched from the corner cupboard. Presently, when she had disposed of the steak and kidney, Georgina told them what Matron had said and Aunt Polly nodded and looked happy, then glanced at her sharply and said, "But is that what you want, dear?"

Georgina polished off the last of the custard. "Yes, of course, Aunt Polly," she said stoutly, and remembered rather clearly that Ned had said that what she wanted was a husband. She turned her back on the thought. "Ned told me that Sister and old Bingham are going to get married," she went on, anxious to talk about something else. "That means that Gregg will get Cas., I suppose. I expect I shall get a junior Night Sister's post to start with anyway, and that won't be for quite a while yet. I shall hate working with Gregg."

"You might marry," said Mrs. Mogg chattily.

Georgina gave her a wide smile. "Oh, Moggy, who? I only meet the housemen, and they're far too busy and penniless to marry, and if you're thinking of rich consultants, they're all married. Besides, it will be nice to earn some real money at last—it's time I did my share, you know."

Miss Rodman straightened an already straight back. "That is very good of you, dear Georgina, but Mrs. Mogg and I are old women. We need very little, and we manage. You've worked hard, the money is yours to spend. Why don't you go abroad?"

Georgina lied cheerfully, "I really don't want to, Aunt Polly. Perhaps later on when I've had more experience—I think I'll stay at St. Athel's for a year or two and get that Sister's post, then see how I feel."

She got up and carried her tray out to the kitchen where she put it on the scrubbed wood table, then took the dishes to the sink and washed up, singing cheerfully in a clear voice so the occupants of the sitting room would hear how happy she was.

CHAPTER 2

ST. ATHEL'S looked grim and grey on Monday morning. She walked into the cold, well polished hall of the Nurses' Home and started to climb the stairs to her room on the top floor. She fought, as she always had to, against homesickness. The contrast between the impersonal atmosphere of the home and the little cottage was too great. She paused on a landing and looked out of the window. There was a plane tree close by, quite a nice one; she closed her eyes and saw her beloved hornbeam, then, despising herself for being childish, hurried on up the last flight. Once she was on duty she would be all right again. But somehow she wasn't, despite the fact that Gregg had a half day. She told herself that it was reaction after all the excitement and was glad that the steady stream of patients kept her busy—too busy to think of her own affairs. Sister went off duty at five o'clock and Ned telephoned to say that Bob Baker would be standing in for him until midnight, and would she let the night staff know before she went off duty. She put down the receiver with a grimace. She disliked Baker—he was on the medical side, which didn't prevent him from knowing all there was to know about Casualty. When she finally got off duty at nine, she was in a thoroughly bad temper, what with Mr. Baker delivering lectures about the art of diagnosing, while pronouncing an obvious concussion fit to go home, and calling a Colles' fracture a Potts'. She had asked him crossly if he hadn't learned the difference between an arm and a leg, and roundly declared that the concussed patient was to be warded, and he had retaliated by refusing to leave his supper to write up an X-ray form for an old man with a very obviously fractured hip. He came at length, and signed his very ordinary name with a great flourish, demanding to know where Gregg was.

"Days off," snapped Georgina. "I'll tell her you were asking for her when she comes back," and had the satisfaction of seeing him look terrified. Gregg made no secret of the fact that she intended to marry a doctor, and Mr. Baker would serve her purpose as well as any, she supposed.

He backed to the door. "I merely wished to know," he stated coldly, "because I'm not completely satisfied with your work."

"I'll repeat that, word for word, to Sister in the morning," she said with equal coldness. "I'm sure she will arrange for you to be replaced by one of the other housemen—she wouldn't like to think that our standards aren't up to yours." She flounced to the door, took the handle from his unresisting hand, gave him a gentle push, and shut the door with great firmness upon his astonished face.

When she got to her room, it was to find several of her friends there with a large pot of tea and a variety of mugs. Somebody had found a bottle of milk and Georgina rooted around in her wardrobe and produced some sugar and a large homemade cake, pressed upon her that morning by Mrs. Mogg, who, although she had never set foot inside a hospital, was firmly convinced that all nurses were half starved, an opinion apparently shared by the young ladies now engaged in gobbling it up, for all the world as though they had not enjoyed an excellent supper not two hours earlier. The cake disposed of, and the mugs replenished, the conversation turned, as it always did, to the future. It seemed to Georgina, listening, that everyone there but herself was on the point of doing something exciting. One was going into the Q.A.s, two were going to Canada, the remainder were either on the point of getting married or engaged.

A voice said, "George, you haven't told us what you're going to do."

"Well," she began; she wasn't sure if she should mention about getting a Sister's post, "I thought I'd stay here...."

"Did Matron dangle a Sister's cap before you?" someone wanted to know.

"Later on ... it was all a bit vague. Perhaps I'll do my Midder." She had only just thought of that, but at least it was a future.

Her immediate future was to be taken care of, though. The next morning Matron wanted to see her. There was no chance to change her apron; she turned it inside out, hoping the stains wouldn't show through, and presented herself, outwardly composed, at Matron's office. She came out again within a couple of minutes. Night duty—four weeks of it in Cas.; valuable experience, Matron had said, by way of sugaring the pill. It meant nights off too, several days at home each fortnight. She brightened at the thought of not having to work with Gregg, and brightened still more when she met Ned and told him, and he said, "Thank God! That woman who's on now calls me for the merest scratch—besides, you're nice to have around."

Georgina chuckled. "Go on with you, Ned," she said comfortably. If she had had a brother, she would have used the same tone of voice she was using now. "But I promise not to call you for scratches!"

They started on their separate ways and as they went he called over his shoulder, "Are you on tonight?"

She went on walking away from him. "No, tomorrow," she replied, thinking that she must remember to ring Aunt Polly.

Night duty on Cas. followed a pattern, she discovered, after she had been on for a few nights. Until eleven she was kept busy by a steady influx of people who 'didn't like to bother the doctor'; toothache, teething babies, bruises it was best not to enquire too deeply into; boils and headaches, cut fingers and ingrowing toenails; they crowded into the benches, confident that someone would do something for them, and in the meantime it was pleasant to have a natter. They weren't in the least put out when an emergency came in, needing attention at once and sometimes for a long time, and they only smiled cheerfully when Georgina or the junior nurse suggested that the next time they had the toothache it would be a good idea to go to the dentist, and that a bruise that had appeared days before was hardly a casualty. After the pubs closed, it was the turn of the drunks, cheerfully escorted by a constable, who as often or not gave a helping hand. There was seldom very much wrong with them, but they wasted everyone's time, for they invariably needed stitches.

After the first night, when there were two or three waiting for scalp wounds to be sutured, Ned suggested that she should give a hand, and after that she added stitching to her duties; of course he did the complicated cuts, but very often it was only a case of one straightforward stitch, which the patient was frequently far too drunk to notice. The crashes followed a pattern too—round about midnight and five or six in the morning, so that she quite often ate her dinner at two o'clock in the morning and had to miss tea altogether, but that was something you expected if you worked on Cas., and it didn't occur to her to grumble about it. She slept like a log during the day, and there were nights off to look forward to.

On this, the fifth night, however, she had gone on duty tired after an almost sleepless day. She smiled at the waiting patients as she passed them and went on into the office to take over from Sister, who was looking, surprisingly, quite different from usual. She gave Georgina one or two police messages in an abstracted sort of manner and told her that Ned would be on duty, and that Mr. Bingham would be available at ten o'clock. There was something in the way she said this that made Georgina look at her carefully. Sister was excited, and excitement had turned her into a very pretty woman. She caught Georgina's eye and said almost diffidently, "Mr. Bingham and I are going out to dinner—to celebrate. I might as well tell you, Staff. We're going to be married."

Georgina put down her cloak and bag. "Sister, how wonderful! I am glad, and wish you every happiness. What a pity Mr. Bingham has to be on duty—it's his night on call, isn't it?"

22

Sister got up and draped her cloak around her shoulders. "Well, yes, Staff, it is. But we shan't be long—if anything big comes in, Ned can get help and send for Mr. Bingham—there's the phone number on the pad."

She smiled dreamily, said good night, and slipped away. Georgina rolled up her sleeves and put on her frills, thinking about Sister and Mr. Bingham. Sister would leave, of course. She went across to the cubicles and checked their contents with practised speed, not because she didn't trust the day staff to leave everything in a state of readiness, but because each one of them did it when they came on duty—it was a kind of unwritten rule no one forgot. This done, she began on the patients. None of them were serious cases, but each of them had to be entered in the Day Book and a card filled in with their particulars. It was surprising what a large number of people there were who couldn't remember their age, thought Georgina, as she waited patiently while an old lady tried to decide whether she was really eighty or only seventy-nine. She was a nice old lady—Georgina suspected that the pain in her shoulder was largely an excuse to come and sit in the brightly lit waiting room and join the others in a chat. She finished filling in her card, and sent her back to wait on the bench for a few minutes. It would be lonely in one of the cubicles, and she wasn't going to get Ned until she had several patients ready for him.

The benches were half cleared when she heard the ambulance. The two cubicles nearest the door were empty; she pushed back the double doors and wheeled two trolleys as near as possible to them, and found time to warn the waiting patients that they would be delayed. It was Ginger on duty. He drew up with a little rush and got out to join his mate.

"Evening, Staff," he called politely. "Got an R.T.A. here. Two kids and a man." He had opened the ambulance door and was pulling out the first stretcher. "Head injuries—broken legs for the little boy—man's a walking case."

She flew to the telephone and dialled the doctors'

quarters and waited a long minute while Ned was fetched. She said merely, "An R.T.A., Ned," and went to the first cubicle where the little boy was. He was still on the trolley and unconscious, and she thought that that was a good thing when she whisked back the blanket and looked at his legs. Nothing much to see, but there were already bruises showing between the splints—probably both femurs. He didn't look too bad, and his pulse was good. The second child was a little girl, semi-conscious and bleeding from head wounds. She had long straight fair hair, hopelessly tangled and matted with blood. Georgina took her pulse too and hoped that she was right in thinking that she wasn't badly injured. The third patient came in on his feet, looking rather white. He was holding his right hand against his chest, and said surprisingly, "I'm sorry to give you this trouble. The children?"

Georgina said quickly, "The doctor will be here in a moment—he'll have to examine them first. Come and sit down. When we've seen to them and I've a second, I'll get a sling for that arm of yours. It looks like a collar-bone."

She smiled at him, her brown eyes soft with sympathy. He was about her own age or a little younger; very good-looking, with fair hair and blue eyes and a mouth that looked as though it could laugh a lot in happier circumstances. She left him sitting, and went at once to the small boy, to be joined at once by Ned. He stood looking at him while she cut away the clothes from the quiet little body, and then at a word from her, steadied each leg as she eased off the shoes and socks.

Ned explored them gently. "This is a job for old Sawbones—" he meant Mr. Sawbridge, the senior orthopaedic surgeon. "I'll get Bill Foster down." Bill was his registrar. "Get him on the phone, George. What's the lad's pulse like?"

She had been taking it while he was talking. "A hundred and ten—strong, steady. I'll get him on a half-hourly chart, shall I? And I suppose you'll want skull X-rays as well as legs?"

She didn't wait for an answer but went to the telephone for a second time to get Bill Foster, and then to send a message to the Night Super to see if she could spare the junior runner; it wasn't very likely, and she was used to managing alone for the greater part of the night. She left Ned with the little boy and went to look at the girl. The ambulance men had stayed with her and she thanked them gratefully. "I'm sorry I can't stop to make you a cup of tea, Ginger, but you're welcome to make yourselves one—you know where everything is."

But they thanked her and said, no, they'd go. There was sure to be some more work for them some time. They collected their blankets and said "Cheerio" because it would have been silly to have said anything else when they would probably be seeing her several more times during the night. They said good night to the young man, however, and he wished them a good night in return and then asked them their names. They gave them awkwardly, and just as awkwardly received his quiet thanks. On the whole, not many people remembered to thank them, understandably enough, but it was nice when they did.

Georgina had taken the little girl's pulse again. It was good, and she started to ease off her clothing. She was wearing a beautifully made topcoat; the dress beneath it was good too, but stained and torn. The child moaned softly and opened her eyes for a moment, and Georgina waited until she had lapsed into unconsciousness again before looking for injuries. There was a dull red mark on one cheek and another one on a shoulder—they would be livid bruises in a day or so. She covered her little patient with the blanket again and started to examine the small head. There were a number of cuts, none of them serious, but needing stitches. She started to swab them one by one, carefully cutting the long hair away from each small wound. The child was still unconscious when she had finished. She pulled the curtain back and hurried across to where the man sat and fastened a sling around his arm and took an X-ray form along to Ned for him to sign. When she got back, she said, "Do you think you could manage to get to X-Ray? We're a bit pushed for staff—it's only just across the passage. I'll fill in your name presently."

"The children?" he asked again.

"The orthopaedic surgeon will be in presently—I'm afraid the little boy has both legs broken," she said gently, "but his general condition is quite good. The little girl has a cut head—I can't tell you anything else until the doctor has examined them."

He stood up. "How kind you are," he said, and smiled so that she felt a small glow of pleasure. He took the form she was holding out to him, and walked away to X-Ray.

Bill Foster came then and joined Ned and Night Super followed him. She ran a practised eye over everything and said, "You can manage, can't you, Staff? We're two nurses short tonight and Men's Medical is up to its eyes. They really need the runner there—I'll try and send someone down to help you clear up later." She went away again, exuding confidence and encouragement.

Georgina went back to her patient. The trolley was set; it was just a question of waiting until Ned could get along to do the stitching. She took the child's pulse, was satisfied, and began to draw up the Novocaine. It was while she was doing so that she became aware of the man standing in the doorway.

Her first impression was that he was enormous. She put the syringe, with its needle stuck in the top of the Novocaine bottle, on to the trolley top, and took another look. She had been right; he wasn't just tall; he was massive as well, so that he dwarfed the small cubicle. He was handsome too, with fair hair brushed back from a high wide forehead, a patrician nose, and a mouth that looked kind. She couldn't see the colour of his eyes, but she thought that they were blue—they were staring at her now, and she made haste to say something.

"Is this moppet yours? If you wouldn't mind going to the cubicle at the end, the Casualty Officer is there—I'm sure he wouldn't mind you coming in to see

26

her." She smiled kindly at him. "She's not too bad, although she looks.... The boy, is he yours too?"

He smiled faintly. "Yes, Staff Nurse, they're—mine." He had a deep voice, but she had expected that; any other would have sounded absurd coming from that great chest. "I've seen the Casualty Officer. May I come in?"

He suited the action to the word and went to stand by the couch. But he didn't just stand; he raised the child's eyelids to test for pupil reaction, examined the small ears and nose carefully and took her pulse. "Has she been conscious at all?" he wanted to know.

Georgina said. "Yes, twice, for a few moments," and stopped, astonished at herself. The man was a stranger and she was meekly answering his questions just as though he was one of the hospital doctors. She shot him a look of mingled annoyance and perplexity which she was sure he didn't see. Apparently he had eyes at the back of his head as well, for he said apologetically, "I'm sorry. You're quite right to be vexed with me. I should have said that I am a doctor. Your excellent young man here suggested that I might like to stitch Beatrix while we wait for Mr. Sawbridge's verdict." He straightened, missing the ceiling by an inch or so. "He will—er—vouch for me if you would care to ask him."

She hesitated. It didn't occur to her to doubt him; he wasn't that kind of a man. Indeed, she was struck by the thought that she had met him a bare five minutes ago, and on the strength of this short acquaintance was quite prepared to take his word on anything. All the same, perhaps she should ask his name. She was saved from making up her mind about this by Ned, who put his head round the curtain. He took no notice of her at all, but said with marked politeness:

"Mr. Sawbridge has just arrived, sir, if you'd care to see him? I could be having a quick dek—er—look at the little girl in the meantime."

The big man nodded. When he had gone and Ned had started a careful examination, Georgina burst out, "Ned, for heaven's sake, why are you so polite? Who is he?" She passed him the ophthalmoscope. "Her blood pressure's normal—her pulse is a bit fast too—a hundred and twelve, but nice volume. Who is he?" she repeated.

Ned gave her back the ophthalmoscope and took the auroscope she was holding out. He peered down it and muttered, "Can't see anything much wrong—better have her X-rayed, though, when she's stitched. He'll do it I expect, while the boy's in X-Ray."

"Who's he?" Georgina tried again. She was used to doctors, who tended to get away from the point.

"George, don't you ever read those nursing papers of yours, or listen to the grapevine? He's been here several times. He lectures us—he goes to most of the teaching hospitals. He's Professor van den Berg Eyffert."

She opened her pretty brown eyes wide. "What a name! Not English, surely. What's he professor of?"

Ned frowned. "Your grammar's a bit sloppy, isn't it, old lady? Anaesthetics. Right in the front row, he is. Knows all the answers." He went to the door. "I'm going to X-Ray to look at that clavicle."

He went, and the big man came back. He said nothing about the little boy, merely, "Shall we start, Staff Nurse?"

He took off his coat and white scarf, and stood in all the magnificence of white tie and tails, looking for somewhere to put them. Georgina took them from him and hung them behind the door, and his tail coat too while he rolled up his shirt sleeves. He was almost ready when she said hastily. "Before you start, sir, would you like me to send a message to your wife? I can telephone her ... you could speak to her."

He looked as though he was going to smile, but he answered gravely, "Thank you, but I have no wife."

"Oh, how awful for you—I am sorry," said Georgina, and went scarlet. Would she never learn to think before she spoke? she thought remorsefully, and plunged deeper. "I mean—it's horrid for children when something like this happens, and there's no mo...." She stopped again, and met his eyes watching her quizzically from the other side of the trolley.

"The young man with them—is he yours too?"

This time he did smile. "Yes, more or less. A cousin. I have seen him in X-Ray." He looked suddenly forbidding. Perhaps, thought Georgina, it would be a good idea not to ask him any more questions.

"Shall I hold her in my arms in case she comes round?" she asked. "If I sit on the side of the couch with her head over my arm—there's a stool you could use, otherwise your back will ache," she added in a practical voice.

He did as she suggested and started to stitch. Two of the cuts had been closed when the little girl began to whimper, and they waited without speaking until she opened her eyes. Georgina said at once:

"Hullo, Beatrix."

The child looked at her for a long moment. "Who are you, please?"

"Oh, a nurse," said Georgina, and turned herself round so that her patient could see the man on the stool. The small face lighted up.

"Cousin Julius! I knew you'd come!" She started to smile and then, because her scratched face was sore and stiff, began to cry instead. Georgina held her close, murmuring comfort, while the man sat impassive, showing no impatience. In a minute or two, Georgina produced a hanky to mop the large blue eyes and said firmly:

"Hush now! If we tell you what has to be done to make your head better, will you be a brave girl while it's done?"

She didn't wait for an answer but waited for Professor Eyffert to explain. He said gently, "You've cut your head, Beatrix, and I'm stitching the cuts together again. I shall have to prick you once or twice and we don't mind if you want to cry; only stay still on Nurse's lap."

She was sleepy again. She murmured, "Yes, Cousin Julius," and made no demur when he picked up the syringe again. He had almost finished when she said:

"I know you're a nurse, but what's your name?"

"Georgina," said Georgina.

The child repeated it. "That's a nice name. Does everyone call you that?"

29

"Well, no, not always."

"What?" the small voice was persistent.

"Actually," said Georgina, "I get called George." She felt faintly embarrassed.

"I shall call you George. That is, if you don't mind? I like you."

Georgina was aware that the Professor had finished his handiwork and was just sitting on the stool, listening. She looked up and caught his eye and frowned in a repressive fashion at him because she found his presence unsettling. She said, "Thank you, Beatrix. I like you too," then laid the child gently back on to the couch, made quick work of spraying each small cut with Nebecutane and then said to no one in particular:

"I think I shall be needed to take the small boy...."

"Cornelis," said a small voice from the pillow. "He's my brother."

"Cornelis," repeated Georgina obediently, "to X-Ray." She stood up and looked fleetingly at the man sitting so quietly. "Shall I find a nurse to sit with Beatrix, or will you...?"

"Stay? Yes, of course. But please ask Mr. Sawbridge if he would spare a moment."

She went down the row of cubicles to where the little boy lay, and passed the young man on the way. He was sitting on one of the stiff wooden chairs, staring ahead of him, but he smiled fleetingly as she halted before him.

"All right?" she enquired. "I'll see to you just as soon as I can—it won't be long now. Your—er—cousin is in the cubicle with the little girl if you like...."

He interrupted quite fiercely, "Thank you, Nurse—if my cousin wants me, he'll send for me."

She blinked at this; it would have been nice if she could have spared the time to learn a little more about the Professor. Instead, she made all haste to where an impatient porter was waiting to go to X-Ray.

Ten minutes later, while they were taking the lateral views, Mr. Sawbridge, Bill Foster and the Professor came in. They went straight to the darkroom, where she could hear them muttering together over the wet films until the radiographer had finished his work and went to join them. They all came out together very shortly, and Mr. Sawbridge said, "All right, Staff, take him back. I shall want the theatre in twenty minutes, please. Ask Theatre Sister to telephone me here as soon as possible. Oh, and put a figure-of-eight on Mr. van den Berg Eyffert."

She did as she was bid, but before starting on the bandaging she filled in a case sheet for Cornelis and got Bill Foster to write it up. There was the little matter of the pre-med. When she got back it was to find that the runner had got down at last; she left her to get the little boy ready for theatre and whisked into a cubicle where she had bidden the young man sit. "Now," she breathed, "let's get you done." She was rolling cotton wool into a pad as she spoke and had eased him out of his shirt when a voice said placidly, "Shall I get a pull on his shoulders for you, Staff Nurse?" He didn't wait for her relieved murmur, but got behind his cousin and drew his shoulders firmly back.

The young man went white. "Revenge is sweet!" he muttered.

"I imagine you don't mean that, Karel," the big man spoke patiently with no trace of ill-humour. He eased the injured shoulder up a little so that Georgina could arrange the pad, and she heard her patient say, "Sorry, Julius—I apologise."

No one spoke again until she had finished her bandage. She nodded with satisfaction at the neatness of it and said briskly, "I should like particulars of you all, please, but I'll get you a cup of tea first."

She peeped in at Beatrix as she passed the cubicle; the little girl was asleep with Ned sitting beside her, writing up notes. He looked up and said crossly, "There you are! Wherever do you go?"

"Round and about," said Georgina soothingly. "Is this one to be warded too?"

He nodded. "After X-ray, yes. Twenty-four hours' observation." He nodded towards the benches, where a few of the hardier patients were still waiting. "Better run through that lot, hadn't we?"

She nodded. "All right. Nurse can make the tea, then

stay with the boy until he goes to theatre. I'll take this one to X-Ray; that'll leave her free to help you."

She went back again after she had primed the runner about the tea, and the Professor, who was standing with his hands in his pockets, looked up and said vaguely, "Ah, yes," and walked away, leaving her patient to answer her questions. She began to fill in the cards and only just restrained herself from speaking when he gave the address as being very near Debden, which was only a few miles from her own home. Dalmers Place, he had said; she dimly remembered cycling through the village years ago. There had been several old Tudor houses in the neighbourhood—it must be one of those. She had barely finished taking the particulars when they came for the boy from theatre. She left him to drink his tea while she went with the child, and wasn't in the least surprised to find the Professor, gowned and capped, waiting by the anaesthetic trolley.

She left the patient in the care of the theatre staff and sped back to Cas. The young man and Ned had joined forces over their tea. Ned said, "Ward the little girl, will you, ducky, and I'll fix a taxi for Mr. Eyffert."

She came back to find Ned impatient to finish the diehards on the benches, and the younger Mr. Eyffert on the point of departure. He wished her goodbye, thanked her charmingly and hoped to see her again, and it warmed her to think that he really meant it. He explained, "I'd like to stay, but Julius told me to go round to the hotel." Apparently Julius gave the orders and expected them carried out. She shook his sound hand and said soothingly, "That's a fine idea; a good night's sleep will do you a world of good. I'm sure Professor Eyffert will let you know how things go."

"Lord, yes. You see, the accident wasn't my fault, but I am to blame. I decided to come to town for the evening and the kids got into the back of the car for a lark, so I brought them with me for the ride." He saw her astonished eyebrows. "I know it sounds silly. It was. Julius wiped the floor with me, and I deserved it." He laughed suddenly. "Poor chap, saddled with four children and me—but he's a wonderful guardian."

Georgina felt a peculiar lifting of her spirits. "Guardian? I thought he was their father."

He laughed again, ruefully. "He's not had much chance to think about getting married. Well, so long, Staff Nurse. I shall see you again."

She agreed lightly, aware that it was unlikely—nearly all patients said that. She didn't see the Professor again, either. He had called in on his way back from theatre while she was at her meal and expressed regret at missing her. She was surprised to find that she minded not seeing him again very much, but she was far too busy to ponder the matter.

She called in to the children's unit on her way off duty in the morning. Beatrix was sitting up in bed, eating her breakfast; rather battered but apparently none the worse for her experience, and delighted to see her. Cornelis had regained consciousness an hour or two earlier and Georgina was invited to go along and see him. His eyes were closed; his face looked small and white and lonely on the pillow, as though it had nothing to do with the two legs in their Thomas's splints.

"They made a good job of them," commented the staff nurse who was with Georgina. "Sliding traction—they were both nice clean breaks. He'll be as good as new in a few months' time."

He opened his eyes then, and asked, just as his sister had done, "Who are you?"

"Hullo, Cornelis. I saw you last night when you were brought here."

He nodded, staring at her. "I like you. What's your name?"

"Georgina Rodman."

"Mine's Cornelis van den Berg Eyffert. You may call me Cor if you like." He added, "I shall call you George," and added again, very politely, "That's if you don't mind."

There was no need to reply, for he had dropped off to sleep again. George went back to Beatrix and reiterated her promise to see her again, then ran downstairs to the dining room, where she ate her meal rather dreamily without contributing greatly to the conversation. She was wondering if she would ever see Professor Eyffert again, and even if she did, whether he would remember her. In the No Man's Land of muddled thoughts before she slept, she remembered that the children had called him Julius. A nice name, she thought sleepily, for a nice man. She slept.

CHAPTER 3

SHE went every evening and every morning to see the two children. Cor didn't talk a great deal, unless it was to ask endless questions as to how long it would be before he could walk again, but Beatrix would sit up in bed, her face wreathed in smiles, and chatter for as long as she was allowed. It was from her that Georgina heard that her guardian had been every day to see them, and that she was to go home the next day, although Cor would have to stay.

"Will you come and see Cor when he's left behind?" she wanted to know.

"If he wants me to, of course I'll come," said Georgina.

"Julius said you would," said the little girl, "but I just wanted to make sure."

Georgina let out a suddenly held breath. So he hadn't forgotten her! She smiled, then frowned at her silliness in supposing that he remembered her in any other context than that of nurse.

She said goodbye to the little girl with real regret; she would herself be going on nights off in two days' time, but Cornelis would still be there when she returned. She explained this carefully to him, and was astonished at the storm of protest it triggered off. Only by promising to write to him every day was she able to calm him down to coherency.

"You'll have your guardian to see you," she observed in conciliating tones, "and your other—er—uncle."

"He's not my uncle, he's my stepbrother," said the huffy little voice from the bed.

She looked surprised. "Oh, is he? I thought that he—they—were both your uncles."

"You'll listen carefully if I explain?"

"Of course." She willed herself to stay awake and interested, while she longed above all things to get a

35

meal and go to bed for an hour or two before going home.

"Well, it's like this, you see. Cousin Julius's mother and Karel's mother were sisters; only Cousin Julius's mother was almost grown up when Karel's mother was still a little girl ... and she married Julius's father and he was Dutch. Her sister—my mother—died when Beatrix was born. My father was married before he married my mother—to Karel's mother...." he broke off. "You do see, don't you?"

Georgina blinked. "Yes, I think so. But you've all got the same name."

He eyed her with youthful scorn. "Well, of course. My father and cousin Julius's father were brothers."

She gathered woolly wits together. "Two brothers married two sisters. But why do you live in England if you are Dutch?"

"We live in Holland sometimes. My father lived in England for years; his first wife was English. Cousin Julius says we're all half and half. So are Franz and Dimphena."

Georgina stifled a yawn. "So stupid of me—I feel I should know who they are."

"My brother and sister, of course; Franz is twelve and Dimphena is almost grown-up—she's sixteen." He eyed her through the ordered tangle of cords and pulleys fastened to the Balkan frame over his bed. "Are you sleepy?—your eyes are closed."

She smiled. "I am, I'm afraid, but thank you for explaining so clearly about your family—are they all as nice as you and Beatrix?"

"You've met Cousin Julius—he's super, absolutely wizard." He seemed to feel that this was sufficient answer. She thought tiredly that it would be interesting to know more about Julius, but as she wasn't likely to see him again, there wasn't much point in pursuing that train of thought. She got off the side of the bed, where she shouldn't have been sitting anyway, bade him good-bye and went, very late, to the dining room.

She got home at teatime. The fragrance of buttered crumpets filled the little house as she closed the front

36

door behind her. She breathed it in and sighed contentedly. She had six days of freedom—time enough to do some gardening, and answer the little pile of letters which somehow she never had the time to reply to. She would go over to Bale's farm too, and see if Jim Bale would let her drive his car over to Thaxted when he went to market—he had taught her to drive, and she liked to keep her hand in. She gave Mrs. Mogg a tremendous hug, threw her hat and coat on to the oak chest in the little hall, and went in to have tea with her aunt.

It was incredible how the days flew by. On one of them, she coaxed Jim Bale to lend her the car and took Aunt Polly for a gentle drive, suppressing a great desire to go to Debden and look for Dalmers Place. Instead, she turned the car's nose in the direction of Elmdon, where Great-Aunt Polly had a friend. The two old ladies gossiped gently over their tea, and Georgina left them together and went for a stroll past the Tudor cottages with their carved bargeboards and elaborate plaster bands, and went into the church and peered at Tudors perpetrated for ever on its brasses. They were very large families, depicted in graduated heights and according to age, on either side of their stiffly robed parents—the sight of them reminded her of Cor and Beatrix. She had written to Cor every day, as she had said she would, and rather to her surprise had received one or two highly coloured postcards from him, each one asking her when she would be returning. She went into the village shop on her way back, bought a postcard and wrote it then and there, and posted it in her turn. She would have liked to have sent one to Beatrix too, but the Professor might think that she was trying to curry favour. She was rather silent on the way home and when Aunt Polly asked if she was sorry to be going back in two days' time, she agreed hastily, knowing that that really wasn't the reason. She had been thinking about Professor Eyffert—indeed, she was forced to admit to herself that she had been thinking about him a great deal—a useless waste of time, she kept telling

37

herself, at the same time making no attempt to check her thoughts.

The following day it rained—a cold drizzle which depressed her usually cheerful spirits. She spent the morning pottering about the little house, and while her aunt took her after-lunch nap, went upstairs to put away the ironing. She had her head in the cupboard on the tiny landing, counting pillowcases, when she heard the front door knocker, and a moment later Mrs. Mogg opened the door. Georgina withdrew her head long enough from the cupboard to call:

"If that's Mr. Payne, Moggy, would you ask him to let us have some more eggs—tomorrow if he can."

She didn't wait for an answer, but fell to sorting the sheets, and it was quite some minutes later when Mrs. Mogg called to her from the hall below.

"Miss Georgina, will you come down? You're wanted in the sitting room."

She ran down the stairs and opened the sitting room door, went in and stopped short, saying foolishly:

"Oh, it's you!" at the same time very aware of her hair hanging in a ponytail and her rather elderly slacks and sweater—the sweater was a deep orange, faded now, but still becoming; it made her eyes seem very bright and dark and emphasised the soft brown of her despised ponytail. She was positive that she looked as plain as a pikestaff, unconscious of the fact that she had never looked so pretty.

Professor Eyffert had been sitting beside her aunt's chair, but he got up now, the low-ceilinged little room accentuating his height, so that she had her mouth open to warn him to stoop, then desisted when she saw that there were still several inches to spare.

She said primly, "Good afternoon, sir," frowned heavily and went pink when his brows rose and his mouth twitched at its corners.

"I was afraid that you might have forgotten me," he remarked mildly, and she frowned again. Surely he must know that he was the sort of man women didn't forget—or was he just conceited? She peeped at him from between her lashes. He was neither. It came to

38

her that he accepted his magnificent good looks as something quite natural and ordinary, and expected everyone else to do the same. He smiled at her, and she found herself smiling back, which made her look prettier than ever, despite the nose and the chin. She went across the room and shook hands.

"No, of course I haven't forgotten you. How could I when Cor quotes you at me night and morning?" She stopped, struck by a thought. "They're all right, aren't they? Beatrix and Cor?"

He was still smiling, and he had forgotten to release her hand. She pulled it gently free, her heart beating a good deal faster than it normally did.

"It is about Cor that I have come," he said slowly, and her heart checked its crazy pace. Of course the reason for his coming hadn't anything to do with her! "You must forgive me for calling like this, but I have a favour to ask of you."

She thought she knew what it was then—that she should go back a day sooner because Cor wanted her. "If I can help in any way...." she began, and was interrupted by Aunt Polly.

"Take Professor Eyffert into the dining room, child, so that he can discuss whatever it is with you."

"I should prefer to remain here if I may," he said decidedly. "You see, I imagine Miss Rodman will wish to tell you of my plans."

"Sit down then, both of you," said Great-Aunt Polly. "I'm all agog."

So was Georgina. She was trying to think what plans he could have which would include herself. She sat down in the little crinoline chair opposite her aunt and left the Professor to dispose his bulk in the sturdy old Windsor chair between them.

"I propose to take Cor home." At his words Georgina opened her pretty mouth to protest, then closed it hastily under his amused look.

"I quite agree, Miss Rodman. An awkward and difficult business, involving complicated transport, portable X-rays, fixing of a Balkan frame, nursing care...I should like you to undertake the nursing care."

She blinked at him. "You don't mean that."

"I seldom say things I don't mean," he countered placidly. "I have given the whole matter a great deal of consideration—Cor is eating his young heart out at the moment. We are a very united family." He gave her a quick glance. "I daresay Cor or Beatrix have already told you that they have no parents?"

She nodded. "Oh, yes. I thought you were their father, so your cousin explained a little, and then Cor told me. I—I have a rough idea."

He laughed. "Very rough, I should imagine. You'll come?"

Georgina stared at him. He quite obviously expected her to say yes. He stared back at her with a self-confidence which wasn't quite arrogance. She would assert herself; it would be ridiculous to say yes in such a weak fashion. She swallowed—then said yes, and added, to justify her weak and instant acceptance, "But I shall need to know a great deal more about the whole thing."

And he said in a tone of voice to make her cheeks burn and her pulses race, "Oh, my dear girl, I thought that you were going to refuse." He smiled briefly and brilliantly, and then, as though he wished to forget what he had said, went on in a businesslike way, "I will explain what I intend to do, and then you can ask as many questions as you wish." He turned to Aunt Polly. "We do not bore you, I hope, Miss Rodman?"

"On the contrary, young man, I am diverted." She smiled and nodded to her niece, ignoring the look of horror on her face. Georgina hoped that the Professor had not noticed that he had been called 'young man' although she felt this to be extremely unlikely. She suspected that very little escaped those cool blue eyes...or, for that matter, those sharp ears.

She folded her hands in her lap, looking, despite the slacks, very demure, emptied her head of the ridiculous but delightful notions which had been filling it, and said in a brisk voice, "Yes, sir," and was quelled when he said, "As we are not in hospital, Miss Rodman, I feel that there is no need for you to call me 'sir' with every other breath."

Her cooling cheeks took fire again. "Just as you wish, s . . . Professor."

She thought for a moment that he was going to object to that too, but he let it pass and went on blandly:

"It is now the eighth of November—I believe that you finish night duty on the eighteenth. Am I right?" He barely gave her time to nod. "You will have Cor as your sole care, you understand, but you will of course take reasonable time off each day as well as a completely free day each week."

He stopped, and turned to look at her, gravely waiting for her to speak. It seemed ridiculous to mention it, but she said diffidently:

"I'm a Staff Nurse in Casualty, and I hadn't intended to give in my notice."

"Ah, a point I forgot to mention. I have not yet spoken to your Matron; I wished to see how you felt about my proposition before doing so, but I believe that I may have you on loan for a reasonable time—it has been done before. If you will leave that to me?"

She went on doggedly, "And the surgeon? Will Cor be under Old Saw . . . Mr. Sawbridge? And shall I be responsible to him?"

"Yes, most certainly you will. Old Sawbones—and do not scruple to call him by that name, Miss Rodman, for I have known him for many years and he has never been called anything else—has agreed to visit Cor as often as necessary, and will arrange for X-rays, special treatment and so forth."

"I see. Very well, Professor—provided that Matron has no objection."

"I see no reason why she should," he replied coolly. "Do you drive?"

"We haven't a car, but I have a licence."

"Good. There is a car you may care to use while you are with us."

Aunt Polly spoke. "Splendid! Georgina, you'll be able to come home each week; it's only a few miles.

How very pleasant that will be!" She spoke in an artless voice which caused her niece to look at her with vague suspicion, but her elderly face held no other expression other than one of gentle interest. She caught Georgina's eye. "Perhaps you would ask Mrs. Mogg to bring in the tea, dear? You'll stay for a cup, I hope, Professor?"

Georgina went to the kitchen, feeling somehow that she had been got at without exactly knowing how it had happened. She helped Mrs. Mogg carry in the tea things and arranged them on the small table by her aunt's chair, and would have taken a cup and saucer over to the Professor, but he forestalled her, and she found herself sitting in the crinoline chair again being waited upon by the Professor, who most certainly would not have been expected to lift a finger in hospital. She took a sandwich and caught his eye, and he smiled and said, "The boot is on the other foot, is it not, Miss Rodman—it makes a nice change." He spoke with a lazy good nature and his smile was so kind that she laughed.

He proved to be an excellent companion. Georgina watched her aunt sparkle, exchanging a gentle repartee with her guest and enjoying every minute of it. He got up to go presently, and as he shook hands he said:

"I do hope that we shall meet again, Miss Rodman," at which Aunt Polly smiled.

She said without a trace of bitterness, "I'm always here," she gestured towards her sticks. "Come when you like, if you care to." She inclined her head. "Georgina will see you to the door, Professor."

So Georgina found herself at the front door, standing beside him, contemplating with some awe the Silver Shadow drophead coupé in the lane outside. However, she had little time to do more than recognise it for what it was before he said briskly:

"Well, goodbye, Miss Rodman." He shook hands in a no-nonsense fashion and added as an afterthought, "Just one thing. I shall require you to wear your uniform at all times while you are with us. Not of course when you go out in your free time."

Georgina, who had forgotten about the slacks and sweater, was suddenly and uncomfortably aware of them again. With the fine impulsiveness for which she had received many a reprimand in hospital, she blurted out:

"But I don't always look as scruffy as this!"

He eyed her coolly. "Did I say that you looked scruffy?" he wanted to know. "I can assure you that my wishes on the matter have no bearing on your present—er—most sensible garments." He allowed his gaze to travel from top to toe of her person. "Charming, too," he murmured.

She gaped at him. This from a man wearing tweeds, which, although not new, bore the hallmark of Savile Row! He was joking, of course. She said so.

"Did I not say a short time ago, my dear girl, that I seldom say anything which I do not mean?"

Georgina blushed. "Oh," she said faintly. "May I know why—I mean about the uniform?" She looked up at him, looming beside her in the early dusk; it was difficult to read the expression on his face, but his voice was decisive.

"No, you may not," he said blandly. "Goodbye for the present."

He went so quickly down the path that he would never have heard her reply, which was a good thing, for her voice had been an astonished squeak. At the gate he turned. "Beatrix and Cor send their love." The next minute he had got into the car and driven away.

Back in the sitting room, Aunt Polly put down her book. "A delightful young man," she said in positive tones. "While you were getting tea he told me something about himself." Georgina smiled. Aunt Polly had her own methods of extracting information—she could, when it pleased her, be a remorseless and relentless interrogator. "He's not married."

Georgina rattled a tea cup in its saucer, and said "Oh," in what she hoped was a noncommittal voice.

"But he intends to marry in the near future. I wonder who she is? He spends quite a lot of time in

Holland—he has a home there too; perhaps she is a Dutch girl—after all, he is a Dutchman himself."

She settled her elegantly rimmed glasses on her small nose. "Will you pass me my knitting, please, dear?" She started on one of the complicated patterns she favoured—not because she liked them overly, but because they forced her to concentrate and saved her from other, sometimes unhappy thoughts. "Shall you like nursing the little boy?" she asked.

Georgina had picked up the tray and was on her way to the door. "Oh, yes, Aunt. Of course I shall." She spoke quietly, aware that she was going to like being in the Professor's house very much indeed, although perhaps not for the right reasons.

Georgina had been back on duty for several nights before she met Professor Eyffert again. She knew that he had been to the hospital each day because Cor told her when she paid her morning and evening visits, but the little boy said nothing about going home and she forbore from mentioning it. When they did meet, it wasn't quite half past seven in the morning. She had had a busy night and was clearing the last of the trolleys ready for the day nurses. She was tired, and because she was tired, she was cold. Her hair hung wispily where it had escaped the pins she had had no time to deal with; her nose shone with chill and lack of powder. As she saw him come into Casualty, she thought peevishly that they always met when she was looking at her worst. She scowled and said, "Good morning, sir" without warmth, and felt, unreasonably, even more peevish when he smiled sympathetically and said, "Good morning, Staff Nurse. You've had a busy night. Do you never have help?"

She was scrubbing instruments at the sink. "Yes, but we had an overdose in at midnight and another at five. They make a lot of extra work on the wards—the runner hasn't had a minute." She rinsed the tube and funnel of the wash-out apparatus and cast him a look full of curiosity, and he said to disconcert her, "Yes, I'm very early, am I not? But the first overdose isn't

44

responding as she ought—Dr. Woodrow telephoned me an hour or so ago—I think she is out of the wood now."

She put the wash-out tray away in its appointed place on the shelf above her head and studied him tiredly. He looked immaculate; not in the least like a man who had been got out of bed before six o'clock on a cold winter's morning. There was no sign of wear and tear, and no trace of ill-humour.

The door opened and the day nurses trooped in, with Gregg in the rear, urging them on. They looked curiously at the Professor, said good morning politely and plunged at once into the early morning ritual of cleaning and sterilising and making ready. Only Gregg lingered. She ignored Georgina and smiled bewitchingly at the Dutchman, conscious that her make-up was perfection and her hairstyle immaculate. She said, at her most charming, "Night Nurse is off duty—perhaps I can help you, sir?"

Georgina swallowed rage. Night Nurse indeed! She was just as trained as Gregg was herself, but in the circumstances, powerless to do anything about it. The Professor wasn't, however. He flashed her a look, and if she hadn't known that her tired eyes were playing her false, she could have sworn that he winked. His voice, when he spoke, was silken. "Good of you—er—Nurse. You allude to Staff Nurse Rodman, I believe. Yes, indeed you may help, if you please. Be kind enough to take over from her at once—I have something I wish to discuss with her."

His smile dismissed her. Georgina found herself walking to the door rolling down her sleeves as she went, and putting on hastily snatched up cuffs. Outside in the corridor he said pleasantly, "I thought that we might as well divulge our plans to Cornelis; that is, if you can spare the time?" She nodded merely, being far too busy keeping up with his long legs. Halfway up the stairs to Children's he stopped and said apologetically, "I forget that I cover the ground somewhat faster than most people—and you must be tired."

She admitted that she was, tried to imagine him

being tired himself and failed utterly. They heard Cornelis long before they saw him—apparently there was something he didn't fancy for breakfast. He was, in fact, on the point of hurling a bowl of porridge at the attendant nurse when he saw them coming down the ward. His small, intelligent face brightened and he thrust the offending food at the nurse as he shouted a greeting at them. "Cousin Julius—George! How super to have you both at once. I say, George, do tell Nurse to take this beastly stuff away—I won't eat it." He was peeping at his guardian as he spoke.

The Professor said nothing at all, indeed, there was a faint smile on his face, although his brows were raised in mild enquiry. All the same, the child's lip quivered faintly; he hunched a thin shoulder and looked at Georgina. She detected artfulness as well as tears in his face and thought with a lowering of her spirits, probably due to tiredness, that he would doubtless be a handful. She took the bowl from the nurse, who went, thankfully enough, at a nod from the Professor.

Georgina put the bowl down on the bedtable in front of Cor, and said with the cunning of one versed in the treatment of childish tantrums:

"You'll grow into a very small man, you know." She put the spoon in his hand.

"Why?"

"Because if you don't eat, you don't grow, and some things make you grow more than others. Porridge, for example. You said the other day that you intended to be as big as your guardian."

"You mean Cousin Julius?" He was watching her under lowering brows.

"Yes, I do."

"Why don't you call him Julius?"

"Well..." she cast a look at the Professor, who was standing, hands in pockets, watching with what she considered to be unnecessary enjoyment. He said now, without looking at her, "You're not being polite, Cor. In fact, you are being particularly unpleasant. You will apologise, please." His blue eyes surveyed his small cousin, and Georgina, watching, could see the affection

46

in them. "Look old chap, we know your legs are uncomfortable and you're hating every minute of lying strung up like this, but that's no excuse for being rude." He smiled, a wide kind smile that made her heart bounce against her ribs.

Cor smiled too. "Sorry, Cousin Julius," he said, all at once cheerful. "I was a rude pig, wasn't I?" He repeated himself, delighted with the words. "George, darling George, I'm truly sorry, I was a rude...."

She interrupted him. "All right, Cor. We know you didn't really mean it. Now eat up your porridge so that we can talk."

He started to spoon the cooling nourishment. "All of us?" he enquired, his mouth full. "Why are you so early, Cousin Julius?"

"I had some work to do here—it seemed a good idea to kill two birds with one stone." He caught Georgina's expressive eye and said on a chuckle, "What a singularly inept remark!"

She replaced the empty bowl with a boiled egg and some bread and butter, and sat down thankfully on the stool the Professor had fetched for her. He had fetched one for himself too; she watched with some alarm as he folded himself on to it, half expecting it to break under him, and went a little pink when he observed, "Don't worry, they're very strong." She turned her attention to Cor and kept her eyes on him while the Professor talked.

"I've news for you, Cor. It's the seventeenth today— the day after tomorrow you are coming home." He put a large, well-kept hand, just too late to prevent the bellow of delight from Cor. "Let me finish—I've work to do, even if you haven't, and unlike you, I've not yet had my breakfast; nor has Nurse. You'll have all this rigging until after the New Year. You know that, don't you? And there will be X-rays at intervals and Uncle Sawbones to see you from time to time. Staff Nurse Rodman will look after you."

Cor put down his bread and butter and stared at his guardian as though he couldn't believe his own small ears. "George? Coming home with us all? Julius, you're

47

absolutely super. I'll be home for Christmas . . . I'll be so good . . . Julius, dear Cousin Julius, I love you!"

The big man's eyes were very kind. "Yes, I know, old man. We all miss you, you know—you'll have to stay in your room; but we can all come in and out, and Miss Rodman will be with you for a great deal of the time."

Cor turned a starry gaze on Georgina. "You'll like coming, won't you, George?" he asked anxiously.

"I'm thrilled. I can't think of anything I'd rather do." She found to her astonishment that she meant it—indeed, her delight at the prospect left her startled at its intensity. She went off into a brown study, watched by the Professor with no expression on his face at all, and by Cor with considerable bewilderment. She looked up and smiled at him, so that her tired face was touched with beauty. "I was just thinking of the fun we'll have getting you on your feet again," she said cheerfully, and was rewarded by his grin.

She stayed a little longer while the Professor told her his arrangements. She was to be at the ambulance bay at four o'clock on the nineteenth, with whatever luggage she would require. He politely deplored the fact that she would be unable to have a full day's sleep, but assured her that she should go to bed as early as she wished on reaching Dalmers Place. He himself would be unable to accompany them, but Mr. Sawbridge would make sure that everything was in order before they left the hospital and had agreed to be at the house by the time they arrived in order to supervise the re-erection of the Balkan frame with its attendant weights and pulleys.

"Why don't you do it, Cousin Julius?" Cor demanded.

"My dear fellow, I haven't a clue; I daresay Staff Nurse Rodman knows more about it than I do." He smiled at her, and she gave an answering chuckle, well aware that he was perfectly capable of putting up twenty Balkan frames if he so had the mind. He got to his feet.

"Go to bed. How thoughtless of me to keep you like this!" His eyes searched her face. "We are all happy to

48

have you with us. Beatrix is longing to see you again."

Georgina said quickly, "Oh, is she? I am glad. I wanted to write to her, but it didn't seem—that is, I didn't care to..." she came to a halt awkwardly.

"My dear girl, I understand, although your fears were groundless. You are the last person I would accuse of pushing yourself forward."

She looked relieved. "Beatrix didn't think I had forgotten her?"

"No," he assured her gravely, "never that."

She said goodbye to them then, and went first to Cas., ignoring a furious Gregg to give a brief report to Sister, and then to the dining room, where, as she so often was, she was the last. She was barely seated at the table before a voice enquired, "What's all this, George—dating handsome consultants in Children's before eight o'clock in the morning!"

Another voice chimed in, "Obviously he likes the early bird." There was a shriek of laughter, and Night Super, sitting with her sisters at the other end of the dining room, raised her eyebrows and smiled. It was tacitly agreed that the night nurses needed to let off steam when they came off duty; she went on with her breakfast, and wished that she was with them, sharing the fun.

Georgina spooned sugar into her tea with a lavish hand. "It's my early morning charm," she explained imperturbably, although her cheeks were pink. "There's nothing like a red nose and wispy hair to enhance my type of good looks."

"Yes. But why choose Children's—it's the least romantic of places," asked the Night Staff from that ward. "Give us the facts, George."

Over several slices of toast, lavishly loaded with butter and marmalade, she told them. When she had finished, there was a silence lasting at least ten seconds until someone said, "How funny—the other day we were all talking—remember?—and George said she wasn't sure what she wanted to do, and now it's all cut and dried. Take some pretty clothes," she added.

Georgina put down her empty cup. "I can't," she

said. "Professor Eyffert wants me to wear uniform all the time."

This announcement was met by a stunned silence. Then, "George, you can't—I mean, you're not a nun or anything—what about meals with the family? They'll all be dolled up and you'll be like Little Orphan Annie in a cap and apron. You will have meals with the family, I suppose?"

"I don't know. He didn't say. Perhaps I'll eat alone." It sounded dull and lonely. "I'll let you know," she said cheerfully, as they rose like a flock of rather bedraggled white pigeons from the table. But all the while she was getting ready for bed, the thought that she shouldn't have agreed to nurse Cor nagged her. She finally went to sleep in the middle of a dignified and rather complicated refusal to do so, instantly forgotten, however, when she went on duty that evening and found a postcard from Beatrix which, though lacking in literary effort, left no doubt as to her delight at seeing Georgina again.

CHAPTER 4

THEY got to Dalmers Place just after six. It had been a slow journey, and a not very easy one, both from Georgina's point of view and her patient's, and now she drew a sigh of relief as the ambulance turned into an open gateway guarded by a half-timbered lodge which looked too small for occupation, but obviously was not, for the front door was flung open and a tall but bent old man, accompanied by a short stout woman, stood on the step waving vigorously. Georgina described them to Cor, who had been alternating between dozing and childish outbursts of impatience, and he brightened considerably. "That's Mr. Legg, our gardener, and Mrs. Legg who helps in the house—we're home, George!" He put out a rather hot hand and clutched at hers, and she held it in a comforting grasp while the ambulance ran smoothly along a short avenue of trees. It was too dark to see them clearly, but the headlights picked up each massive trunk in their beam before it faded into the receding darkness around them, until they came abruptly into a wide sweep of drive which circled before the house. The door stood open; there were lights everywhere and a number of people, but Georgina was fully occupied in helping the ambulance men get Cor up to his room. She was vaguely aware of a square panelled hall, with a huge fire blazing in a massive fireplace, and a great many lighted lamps, and then a broad staircase, with shallow uncarpeted stairs, giving on to a wide corridor that had steps up and steps down for no apparent reason, and a great many little passages running into it.

Cor's room, luckily, opened on to the corridor, and its door was wide. They came to a halt by the bed, the Balkan frame and all its attendant paraphernalia ready beside it. Cor had had his eyes shut, but now he opened them and beamed happily from a white little face.

51

"This is my room, George," he said with such joyful pride that she was able to realise just how much it had meant to him to come home again. But there was no chance to do more than smile at him, for Mr. Sawbridge, true to his promise, emerged from the window recess and advanced to meet them. Cor had seen him too.

"Uncle Sawbones! How glad I am to see you, for I'm so tired and my legs hurt a little; but George says I've been very good and I'm to have what I fancy for supper.... Where's everyone?" he finished anxiously. Dr. Sawbridge wandered round the bed, taking off his jacket as he did so. "They're downstairs in the sitting room, Cor. You see, we can't have them up here, rushing round and getting in the way, until Nurse and I have tied you up again. Wouldn't do, would it—er—George?"

He twinkled across the bed at Georgina, who had cast her cloak on to the nearest chair and was stuffing pillows behind her patient's small back with expertise. "That it would not," she answered vigorously. "We might get into an awful muddle and put you back to front or sides to middle or something, and that would never do."

They got down to work with a good deal of laughing and joking to help along the rather tedious business of getting Cor's thin legs exactly right and the weights exactly as they should be. At length Mr. Sawbridge was satisfied. He put his jacket on again and then stood watching while Georgina lengthened the pulley hanging from the Balkan frame, so that Cor could reach it easily.

"We'll give him a night's sleep, Staff, then we'll get those legs X-rayed, just to make sure that our admirable work hasn't misfired."

Georgina murmured, "Yes, sir," wondering about the X-ray. Surely they wouldn't have to take Cor all the way to the nearest hospital just as they had got him settled.... Mr. Sawbridge caught her eye. "There's a portable rigged up in the dressing room next door—we can wheel it in when it's wanted." He shook Cor's hand

and said, "I'm going to take Nurse away for a minute while I tell her about your legs. Lie quiet, there's a good chap, and I'll tell the others they can come up and see you."

He ushered Georgina out of the door and they stood outside in the corridor while he gave her his instructions. "Don't let his brother and sisters stay too long," he ended. "He's tired, and so are you, are you not? Supper and off to sleep for him as soon as you can manage it, Staff. I'll be down about midday tomorrow."

They said good night, and she went back into Cor's room and started to tidy away the considerable mess they had made, while she listened to Cor's excited voice weighing the merits of scrambled eggs and mushrooms against those of an omelette with a great deal of cheese and bacon in it. He had barely decided on the omelette when the door was flung open and Beatrix came in; she was followed by a boy of twelve or thirteen—Georgina supposed he was Franz—and a very pretty girl, with thick fair hair hanging to her shoulders and the largest blue eyes Georgina had ever seen. This would be Dimphena. She smiled at them all and said in her friendly way, "Hallo—I'll leave you with Cor, only do be very careful not to bump the bed, won't you?" then prepared to retire to the window, where there was a small table, and make out her charts and report book; but Cor cried, "George, come here, please. I want you to meet my brother and sisters—at least you know Beatrix already."

That young lady, having embraced her brother, had launched herself upon Georgina with every sign of delight. "George," she shrieked, "I've had my stitches out! Cousin Julius did it, and I didn't cry and he gave me five sixpences, which is a great deal of money." She paused for breath, and Dimphena and Franz, who had been talking to Cor, chorused, "Beatrix, stop talking just for a minute!" She giggled and was obligingly quiet, just long enough for Cor to make the introductions. Dimphena smiled with a shy friendliness which endeared her to Georgina immediately, and Franz gave her a wide grin which made him look very like Karel.

"What shall we call you?" he asked. "The children call you George, but perhaps you'd rather we didn't—I don't think Cousin Julius likes it very much, although he's never said so, but when Karel told us about you he said you were called Georgina and were the prettiest nurse he had ever seen, and Cousin Julius asked him if he meant Staff Nurse Rodman, and his face was all empty like it goes when he doesn't want us to know what he's thinking."

Four pairs of eyes, all blue, stared at her, and she found herself blushing faintly, not sure why. She asked carefully, "What would you like to call me?"

Cor gave her a surprised look. "George, of course. Fancy asking!" The others nodded.

"Well," said Georgina, "I tell you what I'll do. When I see your guardian I'll ask him if he minds—I don't suppose it matters—you can always call me Nurse Rodman when there's anyone about."

"Of course," agreed Dimphena, "though Stephens and Mrs Stephens and Milly don't count."

Georgina knitted her brows. "No?" she asked. "Do I know who they are?"

"Stephens is the butler," said Franz, "and his wife does the housekeeping and cooking, and Milly looks after the house—they've been here for simply ages. Will you really ask Julius?"

"Yes, of course," Georgina replied briskly. She looked at her watch. "Old Saw—Mr. Sawbridge said he'd rather you didn't stay too long this evening. If someone would tell me how to get Cor's supper...."

Dimphena walked over to the old-fashioned brass bell handle by the fireplace.

"You can tell Stephens what you want. Have you seen your room?"

Georgina shook her head. "No, not yet, but I've not had time."

Dimphena flushed. "I'm sorry—Julius would be annoyed at the short shrift we're giving you."

Georgina laughed. "But I'm not a guest, you know, only the nurse, and there was quite a lot to do when we

54

arrived. Perhaps I could go and unpack while Cor is having his supper."

Dimphena looked rather taken aback. "Milly will unpack for you while we're at dinner, but I'll take you to your room presently, if you like."

She broke off as the door opened and Stephens came in. He was a small man with an ageless face and sandy hair brushed neatly over the baldness it didn't quite conceal. His face had no expression, but his black boot-button eyes were intelligent and lively. He was accompanied by a black labrador and two cats—the first a ginger with a decided squint and the second a rather obsequious tabby. The three animals approached the bed in single file and then stood staring at its occupant, and were only prevented from making a concerted leap on to it by the warnings, delivered in a variety of accents, by everyone in the room. Everyone, that was, but Cornelis, who shouted with delight when he saw them, and begged anyone who would listen that they might be allowed on his bed for just one minute. Georgina saw the mutinous look on his face and said, "One at a time, then," and suiting the action to the word, lifted the ginger cat on to the bed so that he might touch Cor's cheek with a pink nose.

"He missed me—look how he missed me!" cried Cor. The cat patted him gently with a soft paw. "He's Ginger," he explained as Georgina put the cat back on the floor and picked up the tabby.

"Of course they missed you," she said in a sensible voice, "they're just as fond of you as you are of them. What do you call this one?"

"Toto—Cousin Julius said he was a clown when he was a kitten. He's shy." He stroked its head, and was rewarded by a lick or so from a pink tongue.

"Now the dog," said Georgina. The beast, without being told, heaved himself up and laid his forepaws on the bed. The boy and the dog gazed at each other for a long minute. Cor sighed, "Dear Robby, it's nice to be home."

Georgina thought she detected tears in his voice. He was more tired than she had supposed. "You shall have them up here every day—tomorrow morning," she said bracingly. "Now it's time for your supper."

These words had their desired effect. It was decided that scrambled eggs on very buttery toast, a cup of chocolate, followed by a plate of Mrs. Stephens' very special homemade almond biscuits, were exactly what he most wanted, and Stephen, murmuring that he would be back within ten minutes, went away, ushering the animals before him.

It seemed a good moment to ask to see her room, thought Georgina, and did so, suggesting with some diffidence that Franz might like to stay with his brother for a minute or two. With Beatrix hanging on to her hand, and Dimphena on the other side, she crossed the room to a door in its panelled wall. It opened into a room which seemed most magnificent, but also, she realised, as she took a quick look round her, very comfortable. She doubted if any of the furniture was less than a hundred years old, and even older than that— the bed was a four-poster—she eyed it askance; she had seen them often enough; several of her aunt's friends had them in their homes, but it had never occurred to her that she might ever sleep in one. However, she had little time to think about this, for Dimphena had walked ahead of her and had opened another door, to disclose a bathroom which was as modern as the bedroom was steeped in the past.

"Julius didn't think you would mind being next door to Cor," she said, "and you're to be sure and ask for anything you want." She smiled, "I do hope you'll like being here; it's quiet, although we're a noisy family. I left school last term, and I thought I should find it very dull, but I was never more mistaken. Julius says I must go to a school in Switzerland after Christmas—just for a year, you know—and I was so excited about it, but now I've been home for a month or so, and I don't think I want to go at all."

"But you'll have it all waiting for you when you come home," observed Georgina sensibly. "And a year goes very quickly." She stifled a pang of envy, not for

56

the year in Switzerland, but for the lovely home Dimphena would return to, and turned her attention to Beatrix who was demanding to know if she was going to change her uniform for dinner.

"Well, no," she said hesitantly, "your guardian particularly asked me to wear my uniform—excepting in my free time, of course."

Two pairs of round eyes regarded hers. After a moment Dimphena said:

"It seems funny, but Julius always has good reasons for things."

She looked at Beatrix. "Doesn't he, Beatrix?" The small girl nodded, apparently quite content with the explanation. It seemed that the Professor held the reins very firmly in his household. Georgina turned towards the door. "I'd better go back, I think. Cor will need to be lifted up a bit before supper, and then if you'd all say goodnight...."

When they had all gone and Stephens had brought up the tray, she sat at the little writing table under the window, making out her charts in a neat handwriting, pausing from time to time to answer Cor's remarks. However, he soon despatched his supper, and she put away her papers and prepared to amuse him for the half hour or so before dinner. She was uncertain as to whether she was to have it with the family or by herself; no one had offered her the information, and she hadn't liked to ask. She supposed that in a well-run household such as this one undoubtedly was, she would be told at the proper time. She did the few simple nursing chores necessary to her patient's comfort, and then, on his instruction, wheeled over to the bedside a games table which was standing by one wall. It was a charming example of Tonbridge ware, with an inlaid draughtboard on its top. With a little ingenuity she was able to arrange it so that Cor could reach it without difficulty, and after she had propped his bony frame a little higher with several more pillows, they settled down to play draughts.

They were halfway through the second game, which she was losing in a most humiliating manner, when the door opened and the Professor walked in. He answered his small cousin's shout of welcome in avuncular manner and then turned his attention to Georgina. She had got to her feet when he entered, because years of hospital etiquette had inured her to do so when confronted by a senior member of the medical staff, the prim starchiness of her apron bib concealing the mixture of delight and shyness and excitement which his appearance had engendered beneath it. She said, with almost as much starch in her voice as there was in her apron, "Good evening, sir," and got no further at the look of amused irritation on his face.

"Hullo, Nurse," he answered casually, "and for heaven's sake, don't jump up and down every time we meet; my nerves won't stand it!" He smiled with a friendly warmth that robbed the words of any seriousness and went on, "I hope you aren't too tired. Sawbones telephoned an hour ago and said everything was entirely satisfactory." He glanced at his watch. "I expect you would like ten minutes or so before dinner. I'll keep Cor company if I may, and we can go down together when the gong goes." He pulled a mahogany stool up to Cor's bed and sat himself down with an airy wave of dismissal which she was glad to obey. Even if she was forced to eat her dinner in all the severe stiffness of her uniform, she could at least give herself the satisfaction of doing the best she could with her hair and her face.

She whipped off her cap and her cuffs and went into the splendid bathroom, where she spent several minutes examining the great glass jar on the bath, displaying a galaxy of soap under its lid. The shelf besides it was set out with more bathroom luxuries. She examined them with interest and the unspoken thought that they represented at least one week of her staff nurse's pay. It was hardly likely that they had been put there for her use; most probably the room had been got ready for some guest who hadn't turned up, and for convenience, she had been put into it. She went back into the bedroom and fetched her own little hoard of bottles and jars, and got to work.

Ten minutes later she sat at the walnut sofa table, staring at her reflection in the shieldback Sheraton mirror upon it. Despite her pretty starched cap and apron, her carefully made up face and immaculate hair, she felt herself woefully unsuitably clad for dinner with the family. She frowned darkly at her image, applied the merest hint of Yardley's Caprice, shot on her cuffs with unnecessary violence and got up to examine the room. As well as the fourposter and the table at which she had been sitting, it contained several crinoline chairs, upholstered and buttoned in pink velvet; an early Victorian bedside cupboard, upon which was a little lamp of jasper, whose rich blue blended very nicely with the chintz of the hangings and curtains at the small leaded windows, and a small walnut writing desk. She wandered around, fingering the pretty trifles scattered around, and stopped to take another critical look at her face in the Valentine mirror on a side table; its glass was heart-shaped, as was its ornate silver frame. She thought she had never seen anything as pretty and had just picked it up to admire it more closely when she heard the dinner gong. She hurried into Cor's room, with the vague feeling that Professor Eyffert was the sort of man who expected punctuality....

He was indeed, standing by Cor's bed, with the games table back where it belonged and a book ready for the small patient's amusement lying on his bedtable. She hurried over to him, saying in a cool little voice, "I don't know at what time Cor goes to bed—but Mr. Sawbridge suggested that he should have an early night," and was surprised when the Professor meekly closed the book and moved the bedtable to the foot of the bed.

"Then we must do as he says, must we not?" he remarked placidly. He gave his cousin a hand and wished him goodnight, then stood a little apart while Georgina straightened the bedcovers and turned a pillow.

"Comfy?" she asked. "I'll put out the light, shall I, and leave the door open—the bell's under your hand and you may be sure that I shall hear it; I've very sharp ears. Anyway, I shall come in and see if you're asleep when I come upstairs."

Cor nodded sleepily and yawned, then opened his eyes very wide.

"I don't usually kiss ladies," he said, "but I should like you to kiss me goodnight, George."

She squeezed his thin hand on the coverlet and bent and dropped a light kiss on his cheek. "Sleep well, dear. Tomorrow we'll make all sorts of plans." She smiled at him delightfully, forgetful of the man watching them. He didn't speak until they were half way down the stairs, then, "It's extraordinary, Cornelis hasn't allowed anyone to kiss him—other than his sisters—since his mother died...."

Georgina glanced at him shyly. "No, it's not extraordinary at all. Nurses are a bit like mothers—I mean, we do all the things for children that mothers usually do."

He said kindly, "I daresay you're quite right. Anyway, I'm very glad of it; he and Beatrix miss her still. I've tried a governess—a most severe lady; she frightened me even more than the children."

Georgina chuckled. "How absurd you are—how could you have been afraid of her?"

"She used to fix me with a beady eye." He had ushered her into a low-ceilinged room as he spoke, and called across to Dimphena, who was sitting on the arm of a chair by the log fire in its Adam fire-basket.

"Isn't that right, 'Phena? I was terrified of Miss Benn, wasn't I?" He didn't wait for her to answer, but said to Georgina, "Sit here, it's a comfortable chair," then walked over to the piecrust-topped table behind the sofa, where there was a silver tray bearing a decanter and glasses.

Dimphena got up and went to sit by Georgina.

"It's true," she said. "Julius was afraid of her—she used to pounce on him when he came home each evening and tell him how awful Cor and Beatrix had been." She laughed, and everyone laughed with her, and Beatrix got up from her cushion by the fire and came over to join them, wriggling between them on the sofa. Georgina put an arm around her and Dimphena turned to speak over her shoulder to Julius. "You were far more frightened of that au pair girl," and Franz burst out laughing again

"Oh, lord, I'd forgotten her," said the Professor cheerfully. He glanced at Georgina. "You'll have some sherry, Miss Rodman?"

She said thank you in a prim voice, because it made her feel prim to be called Miss Rodman—no one had called her that for years—only the Professor; somehow it made her feel even more conscious of her prosaic attire too, especially as Dimphena was wearing a simple little dress that most certainly was not off the peg. Even Beatrix, ready for bed, wore a miniature pink quilted dressing gown that would have pleased a princess. She took the sherry she was offered and asked:

"Was the au pair girl even more severe?"

"No. The reverse. She was for ever begging lifts down to the village or wanting advice just as I had settled myself for a quiet evening in the study—she actually wanted me to teach her to drive a car."

Georgina sipped her sherry, mentally resolving never, never to set foot inside his car, even if she had to walk miles not to do so, nor would she accost him on any matter, however urgent, except upon the neutral ground of Cor's bedroom. Luckily, she thought sourly, I can drive a car. Now she knew why she had been asked to wear uniform; obviously she wasn't so likely to forget her place. She looked up and was surprised to see the Professor eyeing her in a speculative manner, but he didn't pursue the subject and asked instead about their journey down, and presently they went into the dining room across the hall, and sat down at the oblong Regency table and had their dinner with a good deal of light-hearted conversation. Georgina was seated at the foot of the table, opposite the Professor, with Beatrix next to her. The little girl ate a simple little supper— she had, Georgina noticed, beautiful manners and was encouraged to join in the talk, and despite the elegance of the table appointments and the dignity of the room, the atmosphere was that of a happy family having supper together without formality, although the menu was hardly that of a simple supper. Prawn cocktails and roast gosling, followed by a chocolate mousse with a great deal of whipped cream, was the kind of meal she would have considered a great treat in the ordinary way—it seemed the Professor and his family were in the habit of living in great comfort. They went back to the drawing room for their coffee, and Beatrix climbed on to her guardian's knee and yawned into his waistcoat until he said, "Bed for you, my poppet."

Georgina stood up too and said, "Let me take her up. I—I should like to go to bed too if you won't think me rude."

He got up at once, exclaiming, "My dear good girl, how thoughtless of me! You must be longing for bed and there are several things I had meant to talk to you about this evening, for I have to leave early tomorrow."

Georgina resolutely kept resignation out of her voice. "Very well, I'll take Beatrix up and come down again, shall I?" and was relieved when he said, "Indeed no, I'm no slavedriver. Go to bed, Miss Rodman; but I should be grateful if you could see me tomorrow before I leave, and I must warn you that that is early in the morning. I breakfast at half past seven—perhaps we could clear up several points then? I shan't ask you to share my breakfast, but perhaps you will have a cup of coffee."

She agreed; after all, she was in the habit of getting up at six-thirty most days. She said good night and went upstairs with Beatrix clutching her hand, the Professor's formal "Good night, Nurse" still ringing in her ears. Beatrix's room, she discovered, was down one of the small passages leading off the main upstairs corridor. It was a good deal smaller than Cor's, but its furniture was so exactly right for a small girl, and the furnishings so pretty, that she stopped in the doorway and exclaimed:

"What a lovely room, Beatrix—like something out of a fairy-tale!"

Beatrix was climbing into bed. "Yes, isn't it? When we came here I was a very little girl, and Cousin Julius thought I might be frightened sometimes if I woke in the night, so I sleep next door to him, and when I got bigger, he let me choose the colours I like best...." she nodded at a door in the farthest wall. "There's another room there; our nurse had it until she got married. Now it's empty, but I don't mind at all 'cos Cousin Julius is so close."

She had arranged her very small person in a tight ball, pulled the covers up to her ears, and now declared that she was ready to go to sleep, and would Georgina kindly kiss her good night. Georgina complied, switched on the little nightlight on the tallboy, and went away to her own room. There was no sound coming from Cor, but all the same she went quietly in to see if he was sleeping, and, satisfied on that score, she went finally to her bed, leaving the door open between them.

It was dark when she awoke, and at first she thought that it was the alarm clock she had had the foresight to bring with her which had awakened her. It was, in fact, a gentle tap on her door, and a moment later Milly came quietly in carrying a tea tray. She said "Good morning, Nurse," in a pleasant, soft voice, put down the tray by the bed and added, "I'll run your bath," then was gone again, as silently as she had come. Georgina drank her tea, pondering the fact that there were still Millys left in the world, who unpacked faultlessly, ran baths, and served early morning tea at seven o'clock without so much as a cross look.... She probably had fabulous wages. She poured a second cup and chuckled to herself; it was a pity that her friends in the Nurses' Home couldn't see her now, drinking tea from Wedgwood china while the bath water ran. She got out of bed at the thought and turned it off, then slipped silently into Cor's room, but he was still sleeping, and looked as though he would continue to do so for some time yet. She bathed and dressed, crowned her shining hair with her little muslin cap, and went downstairs.

The Professor was already at the breakfast table, obviously half way through his meal, and dealing with his post, about half of which he had scattered around his plate; the remainder, together with a quantity of empty envelopes, littered the floor around his chair. He

63

had, she noted, made an attempt to glean the day's news too, for *The Times* had been tossed on to a nearby chair. She had a sudden pang of pity, because, despite his calm placid manner, she suspected that he didn't have much leisure; but she suppressed it immediately as whimsical nonsense; probably he liked living like that, and from what she had seen of him, he was quite able to get his own way and do exactly as he liked.

He had got to his feet as she went in and said pleasantly, "Good morning, Nurse Rodman. I hope you slept well. Pour yourself some coffee, will you?"

Georgina removed *The Times* and sat down and did as she was bid while he made vast inroads into his breakfast. She had just settled herself nicely and had raised the cup to her lips when he remarked:

"I've made a few notes of several small points I feel we should clear...." He paused and started to search amongst the untidy heap of letters, until, exasperated, Georgina got up and took them from him, identified his untidy writing on the back of an envelope and put it into his hand. Before she sat down again she piled the letters neatly, whisked a wastepaper basket from a corner of the room and threw in the litter on the floor. As she resumed her seat, she said sedately, "I'm sorry to be fussy; I couldn't possibly concentrate on what you wish to say to me if I were forced to contemplate such a mess."

He eyed her without speaking, drank the remains of his coffee, and answered cheerfully, "Well, it's only for this morning, isn't it?"

Georgina went pink. "I didn't mean to be rude." She spoke rather breathlessly, and felt snubbed when he took no notice of this remark, but began in a business-like way to enumerate the items on his list—days off; her laundry, the use of the car; her hours of duty and what did she feel about being called at night, or should he make some arrangement to cover this possibility.

"Good gracious, no," she said. "Cor's not likely to wake, and even if he does, it's not likely to be for hours on end, is it?"

They agreed about the few remaining points and he threw the envelope into the basket. "I must go," he said. "Thanks for coming down—I hope it didn't bother you."

"We go on duty early in hospital," Georgina reminded him. "It was nothing unusual." He looked at his watch and she said quickly, "Before you go, I promised the children I would ask you if you objected to them calling me George—amongst themselves, that is." She saw his frown and went on hurriedly, "I don't mind, and I can't see that it matters." His eyebrows soared, and she added, "That is if you don't mind, Professor."

He got up. "As long as you are persuaded that your professional status is in no way infringed upon." He gave her a cool glance. "You will, I hope, have no objection if I continue to address you as Nurse Rodman." He gave her a brief nod of farewell, and was gone before she could think of anything suitable to say in reply. She went back upstairs, very slowly, feeling puzzled as to the cause of the Professor's sudden and unexpected spurt of ill-humour. Because she was a kindhearted girl she sought for an excuse—there were, she decided, several. He was a busy man for a start, doing a job that required not only know-how but super-intelligence. Then the house; it was obvious that he had excellent servants, but he still had the ordering of it and its upkeep. The children too, surely a burden to an unmarried man, however devoted he was to them. She had found him rather pathetic, sitting alone at the table, munching at a solitary breakfast and getting his post in such a muddle. She went into Cor's room, and found him awake. He greeted her with a cheerful good morning and asked :

"Have you been up long, George? Did you see Cousin Julius? I heard him go—he always toots twice as he goes under my window. He's got a busy day before him," he added rather importantly.

"I don't doubt it," observed Georgina, "and so have we. We'll start this very minute by taking your temperature."

She had done this and was helping him to wash his hands and face when they were joined by Beatrix. She stood in her dressing gown watching while Georgina combed her patient's hair and remarked grumpily:

"Why can't you look after me as well?"

"You're not ill—Cor's not ill, either," amended Georgina hastily. "What I mean is, you're not strung up by the legs, are you? I shall only look after Cor until he's able to look after himself."

"I should like to be looked after," persisted Beatrix. "You looked after me in hospital."

"Bless you, child, that's what I'm there for, but I daresay I can look after you just a very little while I'm here; just so long as it doesn't interfere with what I have to do for Cor. If you go and get dressed now, I'll help you with your hair if you like, and later on, when I've got Cor settled, we'll do some planning."

Half an hour later, leaving Cor to his breakfast, she went downstairs again, with Beatrix in close attendance, to find Franz already at the table, eating at a great rate. He got up hastily, said, "Excuse me if I go on, George," and sat down again.

Georgina said understandingly, "Ah, school. Do you have far to go?"

He shook his head. "No, I go by bike."

"Will you be going to boarding school?"

He looked surprised and a little shocked. "Oh, no. My father wouldn't have liked that, and nor does Julius. You see, we are half Dutch, and they don't send their children to boarding schools. I shall go to Cambridge when I'm older, though. Karel is there now—he's coming home this weekend."

He applied himself to his breakfast once more, and Georgina busied herself with Beatrix's wants and then saw to her own. They had almost finished and Franz had gone when Dimphena came in, looking prettier than ever. "Oh dear," she said with faint apology, "I'm always last. I shall hate getting up early when I go to that wretched school."

"No, you won't," said Georgina soothingly. "Everyone else gets up too and it never seems so bad."

Dimphena turned enquiring blue eyes upon her. "Did you go to a school like that?" she wanted to know.

Georgina smiled. "No, but in hospital we all get called at half past six," and laughed out loud at Dimphena's look of horror before continuing, "I don't know what Beatrix does in the morning, but I wondered if she would like to come along to Cor's room later and we could play cards or I could read to them both. Professor Eyffert told me that you would sit with Cor while I go out for an hour or so after lunch. Is that all right?"

Dimphena nodded. "Yes, of course. And Beatrix is dying to be allowed to play with Cor, aren't you, Beatrix?"

Georgina studied the small face beaming at her across the table.

"That's settled, then," she said. "I've got a few things to do for Cor now, and then he'll be X-rayed, but we'll have plenty of time before lunchtime."

The morning passed quickly; more quickly than she had expected. Mr. Sawbridge arrived earlier than she had expected, bringing the radiographer with him. They busied themselves over Cor's legs for half an hour or so, and when they had finished, Mr. Sawbridge said, "Well, that's done for another month, old man," and sat down on his patient's bed. "What do you intend to do with yourself all day?"

Cor looked thoughtful. "I don't exactly know, but George says we're going to make plans."

Mr. Sawbridge glanced over at Georgina, who was writing cryptic details of the morning's work on to her chart. "Plans, Nurse?" and she answered airily:

"I've so many in my head, I doubt if we can carry out half of them before he's on his feet again."

He nodded; it looked as though Julius had made a good choice when he had asked Nurse Rodman to look after his small cousin. He got up.

"In that case, I'll not keep you from them a moment longer. If you would be kind enough to walk with me to the door, Nurse, I'm sure I can say all I need to in that time."

Out in the corridor he told her, "I'll be sending a physiotherapist down very shortly—if she explains what is needed, do you think you could manage to carry on the treatment between her visits?"

She agreed, and he went on, "Cor's an intelligent child with an active brain. You'll have your work cut out to keep him content and happy."

"A good thing," said Georgina cheerfully, "because there are a great many things we can do together." She offered no further information as to what these things were, however, and after a moment he bade her good-bye.

At the head of the staircase he looked back. "May I call you George?" he asked.

Georgina's nice eyes twinkled. "Yes, of course, sir. Everyone—well, almost everyone," she amended, thinking of the Professor, "calls me that."

Beatrix came up presently and the three of them played some rather noisy paper games, while the three animals, who appeared to have taken on the duties of bodyguard to Cor, looked on. Georgina let the two children shout as much as they wanted, judging that they would be more easily persuaded to be quiet during the afternoon. As they prepared for lunch, Cor was tired enough to agree readily enough to lie still and look at his books while Dimphena kept him company and Georgina went for a walk.

She changed quickly, intent on walking to the village and back. She had eaten too much of the delicious lunch she had shared with Dimphena and Beatrix; exercise would be both salutary and a pleasure. She was in the act of crossing the hall, when Beatrix, dressed untidily in her outdoor clothes, came tearing down the stairs, calling:

"Please may I come with you, George? I'm so lonely. I won't talk if you don't want to and I can walk very fast—Cousin Julius says so."

She lifted a rather woebegone face to touch Georgina's soft heart. She had wanted to be by herself so that she could think, but she had to admit honestly to herself, her thoughts would have been largely of Dr. Eyffert, it would be a good idea to have company. . . . She smiled at the small girl.

"I'd just love to have you with me, darling. Can you walk as far as the village? You shall tell me all about it on the way, and I want to buy one or two things as well."

She bent to re-button the small coat and dropped a soft kiss on the rosy cheek, and was instantly hugged for her pains. "Oh, George, I do like you—we all like you, of course, but me most."

The walk was a great success. It was a fine cold afternoon and they stepped out briskly, hand-in-hand, with Beatrix chattering like a magpie, her conversation heavily interlarded with references to Julius, who quite obviously had the lion's share of her small heart.

"He's not married," she confided. "He says when he finds someone as nice as me and Dimphena rolled into one he'll whisk her to the altar. But he's getting very old, you know—he's thirty-three. I suppose you wouldn't like to marry him, George dear?"

Georgina looked down at her companion in complete astonishment which changed almost at once to pink-cheeked confusion. She managed a smile, however, and said carefully :

"Well, you know, darling, when two people marry they have to know each other very well indeed, and your guardian and I are—are only business acquaintances. He employs me to nurse Cornelis, in the same way as he would engage a governess or—or an au pair girl."

Her companion gave a small snort. "George, how silly! I don't mean you, only you're not a bit like a governess or au pair girl. We hated the one we had. She used to pinch us . . ."

Georgina slowed her steps and looked searchingly at Beatrix.

"Darling, not really?"

The little girl nodded. "Yes, she did, but we didn't tell Cousin Julius because he dislikes talebearers."

Georgina suppressed a smile. Both children, and Dimphena too for that matter, had a habit of quoting their guardian. She had no doubt that if she were to engage in conversation with Franz, he too would eulogise his cousin, even if in schoolboy language. She sighed, thrusting aside the thought that she herself could very easily come under their guardian's spell.

She posted her letters in the village, and then bought a little notebook with a shiny red cover and some chocolate to eat on the way back and a bar for Cor as well—they spent quite a time in the little village stores, longer than they should have done, so that they arrived back, pink-cheeked and glowing from walking fast, as the early dusk was falling. Cor's room looked pleasant with the lamps lit and the bright fire burning in the wide stone fireplace. Georgina changed back into uniform and went down to the kitchen to persuade Stephens to bring tea for all of them up to the small invalid's room. They sat around the fire, taking it in turns to replenish Cor's plate, and presently Franz came in to join them, with Milly in his wake, bearing a fresh supply of tea and a plate piled with toasted tea-cakes. Georgina, looking at Cor's happy face, decided that family tea, picnic fashion, was a decidedly good idea.

It was after dinner that evening, while she was settling Cor against his pillows, preparatory to reading him and Beatrix a good night story, that Stephens entered with the information that she was wanted on the telephone. She sped downstairs, thinking about Great-Aunt Polly, who could have tripped up and broken one of her poor useless old legs, or knocked her head on the high brass fender she insisted upon keeping in the sitting room. Stephens had said in the study—she opened the door and found Dimphena sitting on her guardian's desk, speaking a language Georgina failed to recognise, but when she saw Georgina, she changed to English and said, "Here she is now," and jumped off the desk. "Cousin Julius wants to talk to you," she smiled, and went through the door, shutting it quietly behind her.

Georgina picked up the receiver and said in the terse voice of one who had expected bad news and then found it wasn't. "Nurse Rodman speaking," she said, and was instantly aware of her delight when the Professor answered in his calm, faintly accented voice:

"You sound annoyed, Nurse. I have caused you inconvenience, perhaps?"

She blushed. "No—no, really. I thought perhaps... my aunt. ..."

He understood at once. "Ah, yes, naturally. I see no reason why you should not telephone your aunt daily. I suggest that you do so."

She said "Thank you" and became aware of a background of distant voices to their conversation. Was he in hospital? she wondered, before applying herself to giving a brief and accurate report as to Cor's day. When she had finished, he said "Yes, yes," in an impatient way, "and what have you done with your free afternoon, Nurse Rodman?"

She told him about her walk and was astonished when he interrupted her sharply to say, "The children are not to encroach upon your free time. I shall see that this doesn't happen again."

She pinkened with indignation and glared crossly at a portrait on the wall beside her. It was of a rather nice old lady, long since dead, for she was wearing a stiff white fluff and a severe little black cap trimmed with pearls. She returned Georgina's wrathful gaze with a steady blue eye which reminded her forcibly of the Professor's. She was still struggling to think of an answer when he said on a laugh:

"Now I've annoyed you, haven't I?"

Georgina frowned at the old lady. "You're too severe," she said with the regrettable impulsiveness which had got her into so much hot water during her training. "Beatrix was lonely—haven't you ever been lonely? She has no mother she can chatter to, and she adores you and you're away all day...." she stopped and added shakily, "Oh, dear, I'm sorry!" and waited resignedly.

His voice came silkily to her shrinking ear.

"Yes, Miss Rodman, I'm at a party—I offer that as a statement, not an excuse. And since you ask, I have frequently been lonely too. You do not need your professional training to link these two facts, I imagine. Good night."

She put down the receiver with a hand that shook a little. It was ridiculous to mind that he was angry with her, and still sillier to feel sorry for him. She went slowly upstairs and started to read *Faithful John* to Cor and Beatrix, but for most of the time she wasn't thinking about what she was doing, but hearing a voice—the Professor's voice, telling her that he had been lonely.

CHAPTER 5

SHE awoke early after a wakeful night. She had gone to bed quite late, half hoping that the Professor would come home before she went upstairs and she would have the chance to apologise, but she had been in bed for quite some time before she heard the car's murmur as it passed beneath her windows.

She dressed presently and went downstairs, outwardly composed in her neat uniform but inwardly quaking; but he had already gone.

That morning when she had readied Cor for the day and had brushed Beatrix's hair until it shone, she produced the little red book. She had sat up in bed the night before, writing in it, and now she began to read the contents to the two children. "Because," she explained, "there are so many things to do each day, I thought it would be a good idea if I wrote some of them down, and we can decide between the three of us when we'll do them." She looked at Cor. "Do you speak Dutch, Cor?"

He gazed at her as though she had taken leave of her senses. "Well, of course I do, George. Cousin Julius and me, we often speak it—we all do."

"Well, I don't," said Georgina. "How about giving me a lesson each morning? I'm a complete duffer at languages. It would be simply super if I went back to hospital and could tell everyone that I could speak Dutch."

Cor was looking interested, and she sighed with relief when he said with a quite wild enthusiasm, "I say, how wizard. What an idea—I shall enjoy that."

'So shall I," she said promptly. "Can you play chess?"

"No," then, inevitably, "Cousin Julius can."

"Shall I teach you in secret? and then one day you

can invite him to play and he'll have the surprise of his life."

"Oh, I say," said Cor, "won't it be fun—what else shall we do?"

Before she could reply, Beatrix interrupted in a gloomy little voice:

"What about me?"

"I've got plans for you too, poppet. Christmas is coming, had you forgotten? We'll make all the decorations, and quite a lot of the Christmas presents too. You can sit and do that while I'm teaching Cor to play chess—I thought we might paint our own cards too...." She produced two more little books. "Here's a book for each of you. Write down all the things we shall need, and I'll get them—very secretly—on my day off."

The morning passed swiftly after that, and when luncheon was over, she left Cor sucking his pencil and looking important, while Dimphena, armed with a pile of glossy magazines, kept him company once more. Georgina had said nothing about Beatrix accompanying her on her walk, but she wasn't surprised when she was joined at the front door by the little girl. "You don't mind, George, do you? You said you didn't yesterday."

For answer, Georgina tucked the small hand into hers. "Where shall we go?" she asked.

She didn't have to ask for tea to be taken up to Cor's room when they got back. Stephens was in the hall waiting for them.

"I took the liberty of arranging for tea to be taken up to Master Cor's room, Nurse, and I trust that is what you would wish."

His little black eyes twinkled at her, and she smiled delightedly.

"How thoughtful of you, Stephens. If it's not too much bother...."

"Nothing's a bother if it helps Master Cornelis, miss."

They ate an enormous tea. Franz joined them earlier than he had done the day before, and between huge bites of buttered toast, contributed rather noisily to the conversation. Georgina wasn't quite sure how it was that she presently found herself sitting by Cor's bed, reading out loud from Thackeray's *The Rose and the Ring*. She had begun by reading little bits of it to Beatrix, who had brought her the book to look at, and gradually the others had fallen silent, until now there was no sound in the room but the comfortable crackling of the fire, and the occasional champing of Franz's jaws as he ate yet one more slice of toast. Georgina liked *The Rose and the Ring*, and was reading it with pleasure and verve. She was in the middle of one of Countess Gruffinuff's most telling speeches when she became aware of a curious sensation. There was no time to analyse it as she looked up. Everyone was looking at the door at her back; so she looked too. Professor Eyffert was leaning against it, his hands in his pockets, watching her. She had no idea how long he had been there. She closed the book, and started to get up, then, remembering what he had said, sat down again, and was glad to do so because her legs were giving her the impression that they didn't intend to support her. She quelled a desire to smile at him, because that was what she wanted to do, with the sheer delight of seeing him there. In any case, he might still be angry. Instead, she sat primly, with her hands, still clutching the book, folded stiffly in her spotless white lap, and didn't smile at all, not even when he suddenly smiled at her, giving her a peculiar light-headed feeling, rather as though she was filled with bubbles.

"Do I interrupt," he asked, "and am I too late for tea?"

Everyone in the room, with the exception of Georgina, hastened to deny this. Within seconds he was sitting by the fire, with Beatrix on his knee, while Dimphena poured out the fresh tea Milly had brought.

"This is a splendid idea," he said. "Who thought of it?"

A babble of voices answered. "George did—it's called a picnic bedroom tea, and Cor likes it, don't you, Cor? It's to save him suffering from ennui."

He gave a little splutter of laughter and looked across

at Georgina, who was carefully not looking at him. "I can't imagine anyone suffering from ennui while Nurse Rodman is around."

She had to glance across the room then, not sure if he was joking. He wasn't. She went a bright, becoming pink and dropped *The Rose and the Ring*. It fell with a thud and he said lightly, "Will you not go on with your reading? I have a partiality for the dreadful Countess Gruffinuff."

Georgina shook her head so violently that her cap tilted a little to one side and several wisps of hair escaped.

"No, oh, no, I think not. It was only to pass the time, you know ... indeed, I'm sure you all want to talk, and I intended to see Mrs. Stephens about Cor's surprise supper."

She got herself up at last, and out of the room before anyone had time to reply, but once outside, she slowed her speed to a loiter while she examined her thoughts. They were chaotic; she had, on several previous occasions, imagined herself to be in love, but she realised now that this was not so. None of the young gentlemen concerned had caused her to have the peculiar feelings she was now experiencing. She reached the head of the staircase and sat down on the top step, her chin on her doubled fists, the better to think. She didn't hear the door close, nor did she hear the Professor's gentle tread in the deep pile of the corridor carpet.

He sat himself down beside her and said in a placid voice, "You see how I have taken your criticism to heart?"

Her heart leapt into her throat; she swallowed it back and turned a shocked gaze on him. "I never meant to criticise. . . . I wouldn't dream of doing so . . . at least I . . . my wretched tongue, it says things I don't always mean it to say."

He studied his well-polished shoes. "I must remember that," he murmured, and when she gave him an enquiring look, said blandly, "I was expecting you to accuse me of being an autocrat in my own home—I take it my fears were groundless?"

She wished she could get up and go away—anywhere, so long as it was as far as possible from the silky voice of the man sitting so quietly beside her. She steadied her voice. "I have apologised once, Professor Eyffert. Of course you're not an autocrat—the children adore you—it must be very difficult for you without a ..." she stopped, and he finished smoothly, "Wife? Is that what you were going to say? Yes, it is. But I have at last made up my mind to marry, so the question need not arise."

He stood up and she couldn't see his face; only if she craned her neck as though she were peering at Nelson on his column. She got up too and he said, "Tell me about this surprise supper for Cor."

It was nice to be on safe ground again. "Well," she explained, "every other evening Cor chooses his own supper, and on the others, Mrs. Stephens and I have agreed to put our heads together and plan something special. It helps to keep him from getting bored," she added, to make it quite clear.

They started down the staircase together. "Is Cornelis bored?" he asked.

"Not yet," she slid her hand down the patina of the oak stair rail, "and I'll see that he doesn't get the chance."

"I rather gathered that," said the Professor gravely. "There was a great deal of hush-hush talk about plans and secrets from Beatrix and Cor. You went out this afternoon, I hope, Nurse?"

He had caught her by surprise. She went pink and lifted her determined chin. "Yes, thank you."

"With Beatrix?" again the silky voice.

They had reached the hall. She turned to face him. "Yes," she said, and waited to do battle, only to have her guns spiked when he replied:

"She's a delightful companion, isn't she?" He raised his brows. "You look surprised, Miss Rodman. I thought that I had made it plain that I am a reformed character—I wouldn't dream of interfering with your schemes."

Georgina frowned darkly. "I haven't any schemes,

and it's absurd to say so," she said crossly. "The children need to be occupied and I have plenty of time; and that reminds me—could they not have lessons for an hour or so each day—the Rector or someone?" she added vaguely.

A smile tugged at the corner of his mouth; his voice was apologetic.

"I hate to steal your thunder; I had already arranged for that—to start in a few days' time. I—er—haven't had the time to tell you." His smile was gently mocking. "I think, my dear Miss Rodman, that between us, Cornelis and Beatrix will be fully occupied." He turned away towards his study. "Indeed," he concluded over one shoulder, "if all your schemes bear fruit, it may not be necessary for me to take a wife after all. And what would you think of that?"

She drew a steadying breath. "I hardly think that your private life is any concern of mine, Professor," she replied as distantly as possible.

He shrugged wide shoulders. "We shall see," he said cheerfully, and disappeared into his study.

Karel arrived from Cambridge the following day—Saturday. He greeted Georgina with an undisguised pleasure which she found gratifying, although it served to show up the Professor's coolly distant friendliness towards her at lunch, when he politely included her in the conversation. But as he addressed her either as Nurse or Miss Rodman, and everyone else called her George, or in Karel's case, Georgina; his attentions merely emphasised the fact that he was being polite to the nurse because he was far too well-mannered to be otherwise.

She went for a lonely walk that afternoon too, for the Professor announced that he was taking everyone with him to visit friends in Saffron Walden, and when she had offered to stay with Cor during the afternoon, he had merely thanked her courteously, and assured her that he had already made arrangements with Milly. "We agreed, did we not, Nurse," he wanted to know, "that you should have your afternoons free and one day in each week to yourself? I prefer to abide by that agreement."

They were sitting over luncheon, and Georgina forbore from making the rejoinder which trembled on her tongue, contenting herself with a look of annoyance in the Professor's direction before turning to Karel to resume their conversation about Cambridge. It was when they were crossing the hall, on the way to the drawing room for their coffee, that she found the Professor beside her.

"No doubt you feel that my—er—despotism should not include you, Miss Rodman, but I am afraid that black looks from you will not alter my wishes once my mind is made up. You will have to bear with me, I'm afraid." He grinned suddenly and wickedly. "Provided I am not crossed, I am the most amiable of men."

Georgina stood stiffly, careful not to frown, but powerless to stop the hot colour rushing to her face. Black looks indeed—she had only been in the house three days, and he was already talking to her as though she was one of his cousins. She opened her mouth, intent on saying so, caught his expectant eye, and thought better of it. She would be in his house for three months—even if he found fault with her on every single one of the days ahead, it would be better than never seeing him again. She said meekly, "I'm sorry, sir, I'll carry out your wishes to the best of my ability," and longed to recall the words when he gave a shout of laughter and said, "Good lord, girl you *are* talking out of character!"

She didn't see him again that day—everyone else came back from Saffron Walden, but apparently the Professor was staying on there to dine with friends. She heard his car long after she had gone to bed, where she had been lying awake, her ears stretched for the sound of his tyres.

She spent her day off with Great-Aunt Polly—she had got up early and done what had to be done for Cornelis before she left the house in the Mini which she had been told to use. The morning was cold, still struggling to allow the daylight to break through the clouds;

even so, the cottage looked cosy and warm—as warm as the welcome she received as she went in, but it did nothing to mitigate the vague feeling of unhappiness she had been struggling to ignore. This feeling grew with the day, inexplicably aggravated by Great-Aunt Polly's gentle questions, which somehow always held a reference to Professor Eyffert. Georgina answered them with a casual air, and wondered about the subject of them. He had come home very late the night before; she wondered where he had been, and what was much more important, with whom. She started guiltily when her aunt said, *à propos* of nothing at all, "He must have a great many friends—what was the name of the people they all went to see at Saffron Walden, dear?"

Georgina poked the fire with a testy hand. "Oh, someone called Sinden or Sinding... I'm not sure."

Aunt Polly gave a little crow of delight. "The Sindings," she said, "they were friends of your dear Aunt Clara before she died. He's a company director, I believe. They have several children—they would be about your age. The eldest girl married a few months ago—a beauty. There are two more girls just as lovely. I daresay your Professor has an eye on one of them."

Georgina threw down the poker. "He's not my Professor," she said hotly. "He employs me to look after Cor, that's all."

She looked at the little gilt clock on the mantelshelf and saw with relief that it was time to get the tea. She was cutting the paper-thin bread and butter her aunt considered an essential part of that meal, when she was struck by the thought that she wished with all her heart that the Professor was hers.

It was after eight o'clock when she arrived back at Dalmers Place. She went in through the garden door and crossed the hall, trying to shut her ears to the cheerful masculine voices coming from the drawing room—there were feminine voices too. She tore upstairs, two at a time, looking like a thundercloud. Professor Eyffert would be sitting in his enormous chair by the fire, she supposed, with the beautiful Sinding sisters doing their glamorous best to catch his eye. She ground her nice white teeth at the thought, and opened Cor's door quietly. He would be asleep, but she would have a quick look at him before telling Stephens that she was back. There was only one lamp burning, and that on a small table drawn up to an easy chair by the fire. The Professor sat in it, with a clutter of papers on his knee and scattered on the floor around him. She saw at a glance that Cor was asleep, and then stopped dead in much the same manner as someone in a fairy-tale who had had a magic wand waved at them. The Professor got up, shedding papers as he did so.

"You look absolutely furious," he remarked genially. "Even in this poor light I could swear your eyes are flashing—I can certainly hear you breathing loudly; I'll wager you're grinding your teeth as well." He eyed her with interest, for all the world, she thought, as though he was observing interesting symptoms. "Your bosom is heaving too—so many girls don't have bosoms these days. I suppose it's the fashion." He sighed. "Cor's already asleep—I promised to wake him up when you came in so that he could say goodnight. Come and sit down."

Georgina, who had been listening to him with her mouth open, closed it slowly and did as she was told. She sat down gingerly on a small early Victorian chair opposite his—it was a pretty chair and surprisingly comfortable, but she remained, bolt upright, on its extreme edge.

The Professor made an ineffectual grab at a handful of papers and allowed them to fall to the ground to mingle with the others.

"Were you chased or frightened or something?" he enquired mildly.

She undid the buttons of her coat with hands that shook slightly.

"No," she replied baldly.

"Temper?" he asked.

Without looking up from her all-important task, she shook her head, although she had been angry—furious—imagining him in the drawing room, and all the time he had been here ... the relief and delight was almost more than she could bear. She folded her gloves neatly and looked up briefly to find his eye upon her. "Shall I wake Cor?" she asked.

He shook his head, still staring. "He'll wake presently—he tired himself out playing backgammon."

Georgina fixed her gaze on his shoes. "Oh. Have you been up here long?"

"Since tea-time, with an interval for dinner—I wonder why you want to know?"

She looked up, intending to make some trivial remark, and decided to remain silent, going slowly pink under his mocking eye. She said finally:

"It was kind of you to sit with Cor."

He agreed equably, adding, "My dear girl, it was no hardship—I happen to enjoy his company."

She had been put in her place. She got up, and he got up too before she could do anything at all, and had taken the coat from her shoulders.

"Sit down again," he invited in a friendly voice.

She took a resolute step towards the door of her room. "No, thank you. I have some..." she paused.

"Letters to write—washing to do?" he prompted. "Don't let me keep you, though I hoped that you would help me with this mess."

He had contrived to look both helpless and lonely, which was unfair, for he was neither. Quite against her better judgement she put her things down again on the marquetry chest standing against the wall, and walked across to where he was standing.

He said briskly, "If you will sit down, I'll pick them up and you can sort them."

He got down on his knees and began passing the sheets of paper to her with an infuriating slowness. Presently she got down beside him and began piling the papers with speedy neatness, apostrophizing him rather tartly upon the virtue of being tidy while she did it, and all the while very conscious of his nearness. She put the last sheet in place and got to her feet. Professor Eyffert had risen too; they were standing so close that she took an involuntary step backwards, only to be caught by a great arm and swung even closer; his other

82

hand came up to lift her chin so that she was forced to look at him. "You see," he murmured to surprise her, "you're not in uniform."

She stared up at him, trying to understand what he meant, and then not caring because he was kissing her, and although she had been kissed before, it had never been like this.

When she drew away from him, he let her go at once, and without looking at him, she went to her room, automatically tidied her hair and then went back again, not thinking at all; aware only of her pounding heart and a peculiar floating sensation. Cor had woken up. The Professor was standing by the bed, wishing him a good night. As she went in, he looked up and said, "Ah, here is Miss Rodman. I'll leave you to her care, Cor. Good night to you both."

He went to the door and turned round as he opened it. Georgina's eyes, bewildered, a little hurt, met his across the room. He smiled and she caught her breath. "I'm glad I waited," was all he said.

She stayed awake most of the night, pondering that remark—it was only towards morning that she slept, so that she missed the faint slither of the Rolls passing below before it was light.

She took pains with her hair in the morning, and still greater pains with her face. The results were most satisfactory and utterly pointless, she decided. He would be gone by the time she got downstairs.

It wasn't until she was getting Cor ready for his breakfast that he made the observation that it would be very dull without Cousin Julius.

"I daresay it will," agreed Georgina, "but it's not for long, and there's heaps to do."

He looked at her indignantly. "Not long? Two or three weeks is very long—it's ages and ages." He appeared near to tears, but was startled out of them by her sharp, "Two or three weeks? Has your guardian gone away?"

Cornelis stared at her with his bright blue eyes, blinked rapidly and asked. "Didn't he tell you?

83

She adjusted a pulley. "No. Why should he?" she asked, bordering on the snappish.

"Well, you're friends, aren't you?" observed Cor reasonably. She didn't answer and after a minute he went on, "He's gone to Holland to lecture—and to Germany and Belgium. He's clever," he concluded, rather boastfully, "he speaks French and German." He looked at her from under small arched brows which gave him a distinct likeness to his guardian.

"Very clever indeed," said Georgina.

"And handsome."

"Handsome too," she agreed woodenly. During this conversation she had been sternly banishing the vague dreams and speculations which had been the cause of her wakeful night. They had been absurd in the first place; now she realised just how absurd. He thought so little of her that he hadn't even bothered to tell her that he would be going away... his kiss had meant nothing at all; no more than giving money to a beggar, or cutting a slice of cake he particularly fancied, or sparing five minutes to talk to old Legg... all trivialities in his day, and all forgotten.

"Are you going to cry?" enquired Cor in an interested voice. "Are you sad? You look watery."

She picked up a comb and parted his hair with great neatness. "Me? Cry? Good heavens, no! I was just thinking—what a marvellous chance for us to get the decorations made for Christmas without having to hide everything away."

It was a red herring *par excellence*—by the time he had enlarged upon the interesting subject, and Beatrix had joined them and added her own very definite opinions on the project, Georgina was her usual cheerful self again, and remained so throughout breakfast, which they shared with Karel and Franz. Karel was going back to Cambridge and giving Franz a lift at the same time.

There was a great deal of talk about their guardian, with a number of references to someone called Madame LeFabre. The remarks were guarded, rather as though the speakers expected their big cousin to appear in the room with them at any minute and they didn't wish to vex him. She longed to ask questions and dared not, consoling herself with the thought that it was better for her own peace of mind if she didn't know too much about Professor Eyffert's private life. They had risen from the table and were about to go their separate ways when Karel exclaimed :

"I almost forgot, Georgina. Julius asked me to give you this before I went. Last-minute instructions or something of the sort, I suppose."

Georgina took the letter he was holding out to her, and said in a matter-of-fact voice, "Thank you, Karel. I daresay that's what it is," and opened it. She would have liked to wait until she was alone, but that would have looked strange; she slit it open tidily and opened out the single sheet it contained. It began, inevitably, Dear Miss Rodman, and ended with nothing but his initials. It was as Karel had suggested; the Professor informed her, in his atrocious, crabbed writing, that as he would be away for some time, she would be expected to arrange the children's lessons at a time suitable to herself and them, beginning on the following day, and that should she require money she had only to contact Karel, who would advance her any reasonable sum. Finally, she was enjoined to take the off-duty due to her. She read it through, and then, oblivious of the watching faces around her; read it through again, very slowly. Any faint romantic ideas she might have still been cherishing were squashed as effectively as though he had taken a hammer to them.

She saw their expectant faces then, and told them the contents of the letter and asked Karel lightly what reasonable sum he was prepared to advance. She had meant it as a joke, but evidently he took her seriously, for he said, "Julius said not more than fifty pounds or so, unless it was something really vital."

She goggled at him. "Fifty pounds? What should I want with all that money?"

He shrugged, and then laughed. "I haven't the faintest idea—I expect Julius didn't want you to pay for anything out of your own pocket."

She nodded agreement, and wondered what it would be like to have even half that sum in her pocket. It would be better not to pursue the subject any further, especially as she had no intention of taking any money from the Professor. She put the letter in her pocket, with the unspoken thought that presently, when she was alone, she would tear it up into very small pieces indeed, and consign it to the waste paper basket, but it was surprising what a number of good reasons for not doing this occurred during the day. It seemed expedient, when she went to bed that night, to put it under her pillow.

CHAPTER 6

THE next few days slipped by, each one a simple routine of nursing chores, lessons and massage, interspersed by the excitements of preparing for Christmas. Georgina had been to the village shop and brought back crêpe paper and glue, drawing paper and Indian ink, and from the children's point of view, the days were never long enough. Dimphena, with unexpected artistry, drew holly and Father Christmases and angels on the cards Georgina cut from the paper, and Cor and Beatrix spent contented hours painting them. Even Franz, after hanging back for the first day or two, consented to help with the paper chains.

On the afternoon of the Professor's departure, while they had all been sitting in Cor's bedroom over a noisy tea, Stephens had come in with a telephone in his hand and the soft-voiced explanation that the master had told him to plug it in by Master Cor's bed in good time for five o'clock. Punctually to the minute, the instrument rang, and Georgina had the doubtful pleasure of listening to four leisurely, one-sided conversations carried on by her companions, and was rewarded at the end of them by a polite message, via Beatrix, that the Professor hoped that she was well. This message, or something very similar to it, she received upon each succeeding day, for the Professor telephoned with unvarying punctuality at each tea time.

Karel came on Saturday, and obligingly took Georgina over to Thaxted in the afternoon, so that she could make a few purchases. She returned to his Morgan 8-plus with her arms full of parcels and he took them from her with ill-concealed astonishment and dumped them in the back, then enquired anxiously if she had finished her shopping.

"No," she said composedly. "I want some plaster of Paris."

87

Karel grinned at her. "Have you found some poor chap with a broken bone that needs plastering? You're not in Casualty now, you know."

"Don't be silly—it's for something we're making for Christmas. I promised the children I'd get it today. The shop's not far...."

Stephens was carrying up tea when they got back. They filled their arms with parcels and hurried upstairs to Cor's room.

"I've got everything," Georgina announced breathlessly. "I'll put it all in my room."

She flung off her coat and scarf and went back to pour the tea. There would be time enough to change into uniform afterwards; the Professor wasn't there to object anyway. Everyone was arguing hotly as she went back into the room, and Karel broke off what he was saying to ask her, "Are you using your own money for all this Christmas job, Georgina? Julius said you weren't to spend any money out of your own pocket."

She frowned. "Look," she said reasonably, "I'm not your guardian's ward—I do as I like with my own money. If I wish to spend it in a certain way, I really can't see what concern it is of his."

They all stared at her as though she had uttered some dire heresy, so that she made haste to add, "I don't mean to be horrid."

Karel said at once, "No, of course not, Georgina dear." He smiled warmly at her. "I daresay you think that Julius keeps us all under his thumb."

She was annoyed to feel her cheeks grow warm, "No, never that. He must be a wonderful guardian to you all..." She got no further, for the wonderful guardian chose that moment to telephone, and she got up and went to her room to change into uniform. The Professor would be at least a quarter of an hour—his telephone bill would be astronomical, but apparently that didn't matter. She was putting on her cuffs when Beatrix came to tell her that she was wanted.

"Hurry, George, please—it's Cousin Julius; he wants to talk to you."

She answered serenely, "Very well, I'll come," and

looked at her reflection in the mirror. It gazed back at her, unruffled and placid, giving no hint of the furious thumping of her heart, or her sudden want of breath. She walked unhurriedly to the telephone which Cor was holding out to her, telling herself that he only wanted a report on her patient. She was wrong. His voice, its faint accent more marked over the wire, said casually:

"I hear you have been shopping, Miss Rodman."

She cast an indignant look at Karel, who shrugged his shoulders and grinned, and replied, "Yes, Professor Eyffert," in a prim voice.

"You are not, I hope, incurring expenses other than those on your own account, Nurse?"

She sorted this out. "No. At least...." she frowned heavily at the pleasant scene around her without really seeing it. How tiresome he was! She drew an exasperated breath and let it out noisily when his voice, quiet in her ear, said, "Tiresome, aren't I?"

She was a truthful girl. "Yes, you are, Professor. It's all very secret, you see."

He chuckled. "I'll not utter another word about it—my ear tingles from the warmth of your feelings. Now give me a report, please."

She complied, and added the information that Mr. Sawbridge would be coming early on Monday morning, to be told in the smoothest possible fashion that he had already contacted that gentleman and had himself arranged for the visit. He went on to enquire about Cor's state of mind and she answered briefly, "Sky-high," whereupon he laughed softly, and said, "I imagined he would be." He went on more briskly:

"Now listen carefully, please. There is something I wish you to do for me. In five days' time it is the Feast of St. Nicholaas in Holland. The children, as all Dutch children do, will put their shoes out to be filled with presents. I want you to go to my room as late as possible on St. Nicholaas' Eve. You will find some packages in the top drawer of the tallboy. Be good enough to distribute them while the children are sleeping." He didn't wait for her to reply, but said goodbye briefly and hung up.

The next day she was free. She went over to the cottage in the Mini and spent the morning answering Aunt Polly's questions, only to find that when the vicar and his wife came to tea that afternoon, that she was forced to answer the same questions all over again. Most of them concerned the Professor; it seemed to her that she had been talking about him all day. It had been foolish of her to suppose that, once away from Dalmers Place, she would be able to banish him from her mind. After the visitors had gone, and she was sitting on the rug before the fire opposite her aunt, that lady looked at her keenly and said:

"You're still happy looking after Cornelis, dear?"

Georgina put down the paper she had been glancing through.

"Yes, Aunt Polly, he's a very nice little boy, and bright for his age. I'm teaching him chess, you know, and he gives me a Dutch lesson each morning. He says I'm shocking at the pronunciation, and I must say some of the words are tongue-twisters."

"How about his chess?"

"He's good. I'm not bad, am I? But I shall have to take care not to be beaten before very much longer."

"Do any of the others play?"

"No—at least Karel may do so, but I don't fancy he has much time at present." She added, because she knew her aunt would ask anyway, "Professor Eyffert plays. Cor is going to challenge him to a game when he gets back."

"And when will that be?"

Georgina got up. "I don't know. He's a busy man, he comes and goes. I'm going to start supper, darling. Supposing I do something to that chicken—I can leave some to warm up for Moggy when she gets back."

She went away to the kitchen, leaving her aunt to gaze thoughtfully into the fire.

The weather changed before St. Nicholaas. The wintry sunshine gave way to grey, woolly clouds and a biting wind, but despite the weather Georgina went for her daily walks, and Beatrix, more often than not, with her. She learnt a great deal about the Professor from the little girl, although she was careful never to ask questions about him, much though she longed to do so. But although Beatrix talked about her cousin freely enough, Georgina noticed that she said nothing that he would have objected to if he had been there. The child had a tremendous sense of loyalty to her big guardian— indeed, the whole family shared this feeling, and she liked them for it. Their affection for him was obviously very real; she only had to listen to them each day at tea-time when he telephoned, although she had formed the habit of leaving the room on some pretext or other the moment the telephone rang, to re-emerge in time to receive a short, polite message which meant nothing at all.

It was dark early on St. Nicholaas' Eve. They had tea a little earlier and Georgina drew the chintz curtains against the gloom outside, and they sat in a circle round the fire, with the dog Robby well in front, and Ginger and Toto curled up carefully on either side of Cor. It was the nicest part of the day, thought Georgina; the mornings were nice too, but filled with the strict schedule she had devised—treatment for Cor, lessons and massage and games of chess before lunch— but by tea-time everyone was pleasantly tired, and the children were content to sit over the Christmas decorations, which were nearly finished. There was, naturally enough, a great deal of talk about St. Nicholaas over tea. Georgina suspected that the only one present to believe in him was Beatrix, but this didn't prevent them all assuring her that they would put their shoes in the fireplace when they went to bed.

It was late by the time she judged everyone was asleep, and safe for her to go to the Professor's room. She crept along the little passage, past Beatrix's door, and opened the one next to it, switching the light on as she did so. It revealed a large, well-windowed room, furnished somewhat austerely with a few beautiful Restoration pieces, and curtained with a rich blue brocade, repeated as a bedspread. She stood in the centre of the stone-coloured carpet and tried to picture the Professor in this, his own room, but only for a moment. He had asked her to fetch some parcels, not stand and dream. She went to the great tallboy against one wall and opened the drawer, and looked with something like dismay at the gaily wrapped packages within it. She should have brought a basket. Instead, she scooped up the hem of her long quilted dressing gown and dropped them into it, and thus loaded, slipped back through the quiet house to her own room.

Everyone, it seemed, had two presents. She sorted them carefully, and found her name was on two of the small packages as well. Everyone in the household had put a shoe in front of the fire in Cor's room—even Stephens had appeared, soft-footed, with some highly polished footwear belonging to his wife and Milly and himself. Georgina crept along the row of shoes, carefully removing the sugar lumps and carrots with which each was filled, supposedly for the delectation of the good saint's horse. She arranged the presents neatly in their stead, and went soft-footed back to her room, wondering what to do with the offerings for the horse. At length she opened her suitcase which was in the big cupboard behind the panelled wall, and stuffed them in. If only she had been hungry, she could have eaten them, but the meals at Dalmers Place were of the Cordon Bleu class, and needed no supplement.

They opened their presents before breakfast—even Dimphena, who was always last out of bed, came into Cor's room with Beatrix. Georgina, already up and dressed, thought she looked like a fairy-tale princess, with her lovely hair tousled and wrapped in a gorgeous dressing gown which must have cost the earth.

Each of them had a chocolate letter—the initial letter of their names, extravagantly wrapped and beribboned —a charming custom which Cor had been at great pains to explain to Georgina some days previously. But it was the second package which contained the real gift. They started with Cor, who undid his with excited hands, and whooped with joy at the watch inside.

Beatrix had one too—a small, dainty version of her brother's; Georgina helped fasten them on and then joined in the chorus of admiration when Franz, in his turn, showed them a camera—a Praktica, he told them proudly—a Domiplan F2.8/50—a piece of information which conveyed nothing at all to his hearers, but which seemed to give him the greatest possible satisfaction. Dimphena's box was very small; it contained pearl earrings, exquisitely simple—exactly right for a young girl. Georgina hadn't much knowledge of good jewellery, but even to her unsophisticated eye, they looked real. She admired them with wholehearted sincerity and a complete lack of envy, and led a rapturous Dimphena to her mirror to observe their beauty.

It seemed rather an anti-climax to open her own gift after that. She did so swiftly, expecting a diary or one of those pen and pencil sets so suitable for the sort of people for whom it was hard to find the right gift. It was neither, but a small, fragile porcelain figure of a girl in a green and white and gold dress, with a little dog half hidden in her skirts. Georgina held it in her hands, speechless with pleasure, for by some delightful quirk of fate it was something she had admired many times in an antique shop in Saffron Walden. It was Meissen, and she had never quite plucked up the courage to ask its price. She looked at the watching faces around her.

"I simply can't believe it!" she breathed. "St. Nicolaas has given me something I've been wanting for months. However did he know?"

The little figure was passed from hand to hand and duly admired, and declared by Beatrix to be exactly right for her dear George, before being placed on the little table by Georgina's bed. She thought about it a good deal during the day. Of course, it was the Professor, not St. Nicholaas, who had provided the gifts, but although he would have made it his business to find out what his cousins wanted, she doubted very much if he would have gone to the same trouble in her case. Besides, who was there to ask? She had never mentioned it to anyone at Dalmers Place. It was, she con-

93

cluded, one of those happy coincidences which almost never happen.

She examined the little figure again when she was getting ready for her walk. She was sitting on her bed, her coat half on, cradling it in her hands. She would keep it for always; a constant reminder of Julius, even if she were never to see him again—which seemed probable. It was unlikely that their paths would cross once she went back to St. Athel's. She fought a strong urge to burst into tears. That vague man of her dreams, whom she was one day to have met and married, had somehow turned into the Professor. He was, she admitted to herself, the man she had been waiting for, and she loved him with all her heart. It was a pity that he didn't feel the same way.

She put her treasure down, finished dressing, and went for a walk with Beatrix. It was still very cold, with the smell of frost strong in the air, mixed with the sharp tang of rotting apples in the orchards and the aromatic smoke of burning leaves. They found a chestnut tree on their way home, and filled their pockets with nuts, so that when the Professor telephoned they were all crowded around the fire, roasting them on a shovel and making a good deal of noise about it. It was while she was peeling the last of the nuts that Georgina had her idea. Beatrix was chattering away in Dutch to her guardian; she was about to put back the receiver when Georgina cried, "Beatrix, just a minute. I want to speak to your guardian," and said in a panicky little voice, "Professor Eyffert, I'd like to go to London one day next week. Do you mind if I have my day off during the week instead of Sunday?"

His voice came back, maddeningly placid. "My dear good girl, take whichever day you wish—have Sunday as well if you need to. Why do you sound so desperate?"

Georgina swallowed. "I'm not. I—I thought Beatrix would hang up before I could speak to you."

"Is that all? I'm disappointed." He rang off.

She took the Mini to London, driving carefully, not because she was nervous, but because it was, after all, a borrowed car, and the road was icy. She parked it at St. Athel's, resisting an impulse to go into Cas. for a gossip with anyone who was free, and hailed a taxi. It was already dusk when she arrived back at the hospital, loaded with parcels, having spent almost all her money, and for that very reason feeling more cheerful than she had done for some days. She drove back as fast as she dared, for she had said that she would be back in time for tea with Cor and she hated to disappoint him. As it was, they were half-way through the meal by the time she reached her room. She tossed her parcels on to the eighteenth-century giltwood chair by the window, and then took them off its beautiful gros point seat. She wasn't sure, but probably it was a valuable antique. She arranged her parcels tidily on the chest of drawers instead, and was on her way to Cor's room as the telephone rang. She went and sat quietly by the fire with her cup of tea, wondering if the Professor would want to speak to her. Apparently he didn't, for after a few minutes he rang off, without even so much as his usual formal message.

She waited until she went to bed before opening her purchases. Most of them were presents for Christmas, but some of them were for herself. The largest box contained a dress—a long-skirted dream of a dress, of dark green velvet, with narrow sleeves and a high neck banded with white organdie—a feminine version of a clerical collar, its demureness accentuated by the white organdie wristbands. It had cost a great deal of money, and she wasn't quite sure why she had bought it. She had told herself that she needed a dress for the Hospital Ball after Christmas and she tried it on, refusing to listen to the wilful small voice tucked away in the back of her head, which suggested that there might be an opportunity to wear it before then. She had bought velvet slippers too, and for good measure, another lipstick. She tried them all on before she went to bed, then hung the dress in the magnificently fitted cupboard in the wall. In all likelihood it would stay there until she left Dalmers Place.

The next few days were busy ones. Mr. Sawbridge

came, followed by the physiotherapist and the radiographer. The Professor had said he would be home in two days' time, and there were only five days left before Christmas. The decorations were almost finished; they had only to be sorted into boxes, ready to be put up on Christmas Eve. The tree had been installed in the drawing room by old Legg, and Mrs. Stephens sent up vast quantities of mince pies each tea-time.

Karel was home too, and Franz was on holiday from school—the old house was alive with a cheerful bustle. It began to snow the day before the Professor was due back. Georgina got Milly to sit with Cor while they all went outside and built a snowman, and afterwards, at Beatrix's urgent request, had a tremendous battle with snowballs, which left them glowing and famished. When they went back indoors and Georgina saw Cor's rebellious face against the pillows, she went to him and put a comforting arm around him and said:

"You may not be as big as your guardian, Cor, not in size, but you're a real big man just the same. If you weren't I would never have been able to go outside with the others, because you would have made a fuss, and that would have made it unpleasant for everybody, wouldn't it? We each threw a snowball for you, and put one of your caps on the snowman, and here's Franz with something for you." The something was a plastic bucket, filled with snow, which Cor, suitably protected, made into snowballs for Franz and Karel to hurl out of the window; this restored his good humour to such an extent that Georgina heard him repeating to his brother what she had said, with a few embellishments which he and thought up for himself.

Karel was going out to dinner, and when the rest of them had dined they went back to Cor's room. It was barely half past eight, and past the children's bedtime, but Georgina saw that they were both far too excited to sleep.

"I'm going to wash my hair," she announced. "I'll do it now, and then how about singing some carols while I'm drying it?" Her suggestion was greeted with enthusiasm, and Dimphena made it easier by saying that she wanted to wash her hair too, anyway. Half an hour later they were sitting by the fire again, the girls in their dressing growns, and Beatrix ensconced firmly on Georgina's lap. There was a carol programme on Cor's radio and they were all singing with gusto, but presently the programme ended and Georgina said, "I wish we had a piano, then we could sing all we wanted."

Dimphena, who was brushing her hair on the opposite side of the fire, looked up. "But we have! Not the one in the drawing room—there's one in the schoolroom at the end of the corridor—it's on casters."

It was no sooner said than done. With Franz's help, the piano was installed; five minutes later Georgina was seated at it, playing 'The First Nowell' with great verve and dash, and leading the singing in a rather nice soprano. They were singing so heartily that they failed to hear the car crunching through the snow on the drive below; they were still singing when the Professor opened the door. At the sight of him they stopped with the abruptness of a cut of the scissors through tape. They surged to meet him, laughing and talking and exclaiming; telling him everything at once. Georgina sat at the piano, watching him as he greeted each of them in turn while his eyes swept lazily around the room, noting the untidy heaps of decorations overflowing their boxes, the gay wrapping paper, the labels and string, the Christmas cards festooning the Balkan frame over Cor's bed, the cats and Robby crossing the room to wreathe themselves around his legs, the abandoned towels from the hair-drying session. At the piano he blinked, and then eyebrows lifted, gave her a long look. She reddened under it, conscious that a dressing gown and hair hanging anyhow were the antithesis of the uniform he had requested her to wear at all times. He started towards her and she longed to turn and run. He would be bitingly polite and she would be shattered. . . . But he said, to surprise her utterly:

"I have been looking forward to coming home—I didn't realise how much until the moment I entered this room."

She stared at him while she got her breath. "It's

Christmas—the children have been so good, I thought an extra hour would be fun for them—and it's my fault the piano is here. I hope you aren't too annoyed."

He gave her a half smile and said without annoyance, "It amazes me how you contrive to make me out to be an ogre. Why should I object to the children—or you—being happy?"

His blue eyes searched her face and his smile widened. "I can't think how we ever managed without you...."

The others had closed in around them; she looked round at their glowing faces. "You're not an ogre, Professor. I—I think I was surprised."

Cor's voice broke in before she could say more.

"Cousin Julius, you haven't seen anything, have you? I mean anything strange in this room?"

He sounded apprehensive. His guardian stopped his calm study of Georgina and wandered over to the bed. "No," he answered readily. "Should I have done so?" He looked round him vaguely. "It all looks much as usual." He was answered by a good deal of laughter and a babel of voices, each offering an explanation, which didn't cease until he told Franz to go down to the hall and bring up the packages he would find there.

There was something for each of them in gay, beribboned boxes. Georgina opened hers to find a small Delft blue bowl full of budding crocuses. She voiced her thanks shyly and he cut them short with a quiet, "Only a trifle, Miss Rodman." She thought he was going to say something else, but Dimphena asked him just then if he would like a meal.

He put a large arm across her shoulders. "No, thanks, Phena. I dined on the way."

"Ooh! A date?"

Georgina looked up and saw that he was watching her; he didn't take his eyes away as he answered carelessly, "Yes, I suppose you might call it that.... Nurse, would you be good enough to give me a few minutes of your time in the morning? If you would breakfast with me—or a cup of coffee if you prefer—there are several things I wish to discuss."

She said, "Yes. Yes, of course, Professor," and he turned away to talk to Cor just as Stephens came in with a tray loaded with steaming mugs, which he set down on the chest, saying, "The hot milk, Nurse," and glided away again, with a small discreet smile. Georgina busied herself handing the mugs round—Stephens had put an extra one on the tray, but she wasn't sure if the Professor would fancy it after the good dinner he had doubtless eaten; she was about to ask him when he asked:

"What on earth are you all drinking?"

"Hot milk." She spoke in a matter-of-fact voice. "Perhaps you would like...?"

He interrupted her. "Er—no, milk isn't a favourite drink of mine." He went to the door and waved a casual hand. *"Wel te rusten."*

They chorused a reply, and when he had gone, Georgina said smugly: "I know what that meant in English," and was at once deflated by Cor who said scathingly, "I should jolly well hope so, George, because I've told you and told you, and you must have remembered some of it."

"Indeed I do," she replied, "but this isn't the time of day for lessons. Bed, everyone, and *Wel te rusten* to you all."

It was snowing again in the morning. She went quickly through the quiet house to where the Professor was breakfasting; it reminded her of her first morning, for the post, ten times greater this morning by reason of it being Christmas, was strewn around him, rather as though a gale had blown it haphazard through one of the latticed windows. He got up, sending a fresh shower of envelopes on to the floor, and said:

"Good morning—nice of you to get up so early. Shall it be coffee?"

She nodded and said good morning, following it up with the observation that it was snowing and he would be advised to leave in good time if he wished to reach London in time to get any work done. She was pouring coffee from the small Georgian coffee pot as she spoke, and so failed to see the amusement on his face, but when he thanked her for her solicitude, it was with such meekness that she looked at him with sudden suspicion, to encounter a mild stare which betrayed no inkling of his thoughts.

When he spoke it was with unwonted briskness. "Cor's legs—excellent, you'll be pleased to hear—a first class union of both femurs. If there's no hitch, he should be up on his feet by the first week in February. How do the lessons go?"

She answered earnestly, "Very well. He and Beatrix have both worked hard—Mr. Coppin won't be coming again until the first week in January. He's got too much church work to do." She hesitated. "I expect you know that already."

"We discussed it before I went away. I told him to make his own arrangements and tell you." He buttered a finger of toast and heaped it with marmalade. "What about you?" he asked.

She looked at him stupidly. "Me?"

He sighed. "Christmas, my dear girl. Don't you want extra days off?"

She looked down at her cup. "Of course, you would like me to go away for Christmas," she stated flatly.

He gazed at her in some astonishment, his coffee cup half way to his lips. "Now why in the name of thunder do you say that?" he wanted to know. "Of course we don't want you to go away for Christmas, but it hardly seems fair to keep you when you may have long-cherished plans of your own."

"Well, I haven't," said Georgina shortly. "Ever since I've worked in hospital, Great-Aunt Polly has spent the day with friends at Elmdon. It's rather difficult to get Christmas free in hospital," she added, just in case he didn't know.

"In that case, Nurse, I should be glad if you would stay. But please feel free to go to your home during the holidays. We shall all be here; it would be a poor set-up if we can't contrive to look after Cor for a few hours."

But she still hesitated, uncertain as to whether he was being kind or whether he really wanted her. Her thoughts were reflected in her face, for he said, his voice at its most placid:

"The children are very fond of you; and I mean all four of them. Karel is half inclined to fall in love with you, and I consider you an excellent nurse. What more do you want?"

What more indeed? Georgina preferred not to answer that question, not even to herself. "Nothing," she replied mendaciously.

He nodded. "That's settled, then. How is Cor's appetite?"

They were on safe ground again. She answered the rest of his questions in a brisk, pleasant voice, mindful that she was the nurse, on duty, as that was evidently how he thought of her. If he ever did think of her.

The Professor pushed back his chair and stretched out his long legs before him. "When is your next day off?"

"The day after tomorrow..." she broke off as he opened another letter and allowed its envelope to flutter to the carpet. "Why are you so untidy?" she asked in a vexed fashion. "You only have to put the waste paper basket by your chair."

She got up and did so as she spoke, and picked up the scattered envelopes and pushed them into it rather impatiently.

"I forget. And Stephens or Milly always clear up the mess and never say a word."

"Meaning that I do?" She was on her knees, picking up cards and letters and bills. He looked around him. "You're very good at it. I suppose you wouldn't consider—er—just over Christmas?"

She laughed. "Yes, of course. Dimphena answers the cards, doesn't she? That leaves the invitations and the bills and your private letters."

She was reducing chaos to four orderly piles as she spoke, and handed him the last pile. He stuffed them into his pocket and got to his feet.

"Would you put the rest on my desk? Dimphena can see to the cards and I'll go through the bills this evening."

"And the invitations," she prompted, and watched his frown. "If it helps, you could write Yes or No on the cards and I could fill them in and address the envelopes. Dimphena is awfully busy, and I have plenty of time."

He stood close to her, looking down without expression into her upturned face. "That's kind of you—but wouldn't it be transgressing your nursing rules or whatever it is you obey?"

Georgina's gentle curves took on a militant appearance. "We don't have those kind of rules, Professor. We make ourselves useful. If you don't wish to accept my offer, you have only to say so."

She tossed her head, and a few tendrils of hair escaped and floated about her ears. She had opened her mouth to deliver a further crushing remark when he caught her by the shoulders.

"What a delightful creature you are!" he remarked with a laugh in his voice, and kissed her fleetingly on her mouth. "Remind me to invite you for next Christmas; you can help me with my correspondence again."

He went away without another word, leaving her standing in the middle of the lovely old room. He was quite out of hearing when she said in a forlorn voice, "You won't need me next Christmas; you'll have a wife."

CHAPTER 7

GEORGINA got up earlier than usual on her day off. She had looked out of her window when she got out of bed and had seen the first few desultory snowflakes falling from the black early morning sky. She had intended taking the Mini over to Aunt Polly's, but now she wasn't so sure. There was a bus from the village, though; she could go to Thaxted and change there. It would take much longer, but if she didn't go Aunt Polly and Mrs. Mogg wouldn't get their presents. She went downstairs and had the post half sorted by the time the Professor came down, with Robby at his heels. He wished her good morning, and went over to the sideboard, saying as he went:

"Finished? Good. You had better have breakfast now, then you can make an early start for Chickney."

He came back to the table with a bowl of porridge in each hand, and said firmly, "Sit down, Nurse. You shouldn't be here anyway, you know. It's your day off ..." he broke off. "You're in uniform. Why?"

Georgina spooned brown sugar on to her porridge and replied in a composed voice, "I remember very clearly your wishes that I should wear uniform at all times while I was here. I'm going by bus today. It doesn't leave the village until almost ten o'clock. I shall have plenty of time to see to Cor's breakfast and still have leisure to catch the bus, dressed, I hope, like any other woman of my age. As I am still—on duty, I am wearing uniform, as you requested."

She began to eat her breakfast, watching him through her long lashes. He would have to make some sort of a reply. He didn't. Instead he said blandly, "You're being ridiculous about the bus. I apprehend that you are not taking the Mini because it is mine and you might skid or something of that sort. In that case,

Karel shall take you, and bring you back when you wish."

She stared at him. "Indeed he won't. Whatever next? I expect he's got his day planned; why should he waste half of it taking me when there's a perfectly good bus service...."

"Three buses a day, I believe?" he queried silkily. A corner of his mouth twitched and she saw it, so that her hand shook a little with temper as she poured the coffee. He took the pot from her and said infuriatingly, "Tut-tut, Miss Rodman, you are being what my old nanny would call a crosspatch. Karel will be delighted to take you and well you know it. Had it not entered your head to ask him?"

He passed her the coffee, offered her sugar and cream, and asked,

"Eggs and bacon?" and went over to the sideboard again to peer under the lids of the dishes set out on the hotplate.

She surveyed his back with a kindling eye and said somewhat belatedly:

"No, of course I didn't. I should no more dream of asking him than...." She stopped, went red, drank coffee far too hot and choked.

He put a plate down before her, patted her absent-mindedly on the back and took his own seat again. "Me?" he asked. "No, I don't imagine you would—but then I'm not Karel, am I?" He picked up his knife and fork. "I must congratulate you on teaching Cor to play a very creditable game of chess."

She replied suitably, most of her mind occupied with his previous remark. Just what had he meant, or hadn't he meant anything at all? His voice broke into her seething thoughts.

"You're not attending, Miss Rodman."

She raised her eyes to his and asked, not in the least meaning to:

"How did you—that is—St. Nicholaas know that I wanted that china figure—the girl with the dog?"

He took a slice of toast and then pointed it accusingly at her.

"Why must you always have an answer for everything? Can you not, just for once, believe in fairy-tales?"

He buttered his toast and she refilled his cup and answered seriously:

"I should like to very much—only there aren't many fairy-tales in hospital, you know, and after a while you forget about them."

"Then don't," said the Professor. He picked up the pile of cards before him. "These aren't all invitations, are they? Can I get out of any of them? Phena likes to go to them all, but Karel's home now, he can take her—I can only bear a certain amount of this modern dancing. I get lonely dancing by myself," he added plaintively, and Georgina laughed.

"How ridiculous you are," she chuckled. "It's the fashion. But I know what you mean—I'd rather dance with someone too."

He raised an eyebrow. "Miss Rodman, do not tell me that at last we agree wholeheartedly about something outside our own small world of hospital?"

He grinned at her and got to his feet. "You had better go and transform yourself into—what was it—a normal woman of your age, because I am going up to see Karel before I go."

He was right, of course. Karel was delighted to take her. They bundled her packages into the back of the Morgan and he added a large square box of his own, which, when Georgina queried it, she was told was none of her business. The roads were bad, but passable, and Karel drove well. They enjoyed the trip and arrived at the cottage in the highest possible spirits. Karel got out and started to unload the parcels. "You go on in," he suggested, "and I'll bring these along."

He followed her into the warmth of the little hall, put his burden down and went back for the square box, and after introductions had been made, presented it to Great-Aunt Polly. "From Julius," he explained. "There's a card inside somewhere."

Aunt Polly went a delicate pink. "How very kind!" she breathed. "Georgina, undo it, dear, will you?"

Georgina did as she was asked, revealing half a dozen

bottles of champagne. They looked festive and luxurious, and although the name on the bottles meant nothing to her, she was sure that the Professor would have sent only the best that was to be had.

Karel stayed for coffee and showed no disposition to hurry away. In the end he went, promising to return about eight o'clock that evening. When he had gone, Aunt Polly poured herself a second cup and remarked:

"What a nice boy—let's hope that he grows into just such a man as his cousin. He seems very fond of you, dear." Her guileless eye met Georgina's and she smiled. "He's rather young," she observed.

Georgina selected a chocolate biscuit. "Yes, Aunt dear. He's twenty-two, and he is, as you say, very young. He's also a perfect dear, but a bit hasty and impulsive. He's clever—he intends to be an orthopaedic surgeon. He and Julius...."

"Julius?"

She blushed and frowned at her carelessness. She would have to guard her tongue. "Everyone calls the Professor Julius, and I'm afraid I've got into the habit of doing it myself."

"I can't think why you don't," said her aunt surprisingly. "It's very—er—stuffy to keep on with Professor this and Doctor that."

Georgina felt shocked; she was about to demolish another biscuit, but held it arrested in mid-air while she tried to explain to her aunt.

"Well, I daresay if the Professor and I had met in an office or in someone's house or something like that, we should call each other...." she paused. "It's no use, Aunt Polly. He always calls me Nurse or Miss Rodman—he wouldn't call a nurse by her christian name in hospital, you see. It just isn't done—at least, not often, and he wants to keep our—our relationship the same as though we were working on a ward, or Cas." She added helplessly, "He's very anxious that I should be a nurse and not a girl." She remembered the night he had returned from Holland and had kissed her; she had been a girl all right then, just for a few minutes, but it wasn't much use brooding over that.

She gave her aunt a brilliant smile and plunged into a colourful account of life at Dalmers Place. It was lunch time by the time she had finished and she went into the kitchen to help Moggy dish up and to make sure that all the arrangements had been made for her aunt to go to Elmdon on Christmas Day. They opened one of the bottles of champagne and got a little festive, and presently Aunt Polly went to sleep and Georgina bundled Mrs. Moggs up to her room to take a nap too, before going into the kitchen to wash up and get the tea tray ready before going back to sit by the fire and read the Christmas cards and the letters, and presently, to dream a little.

Karel arrived very punctually and stayed for half an hour, drinking Moggy's hot chocolate and eating mince pies. He got up at length, saying:

"If I stay any longer, you won't have a pie left in the house. I ate an excellent dinner too, though only the kids were there. Phena has gone off with some fellow or other to the Peachems' party, and Julius has his own stamping ground in town."

He bade Great-Aunt Polly goodbye, and Mrs. Moggs too, then waited patiently while Georgina made her somewhat more protracted ones. On the way back he said, "A pity we can't have an evening out ourselves. I don't suppose you'd like to go anywhere?" he added hopefully.

She smiled at him in the darkness of the car. "How nice of you to ask me, Karel. I should have loved it, but I can't really, can I? I haven't spoilt your evening, have I? I mean, you could have gone off to a party or dinner or something if you hadn't had to come for me."

"Much rather come for you, Georgina," he answered gruffly. "I like your aunt—perhaps I could take you over next time you go?"

"Yes, of course, if you're home—and stay to lunch if you've nothing better to do."

"I say—rather not! I shall keep you to that."

He cheered up after that, and they arrived back in great spirits and went straight to Cor's room. The little boy was still awake and inclined to be peevish. Georgina took one look at him.

"Gosh, I'm tired. I think I shall go to bed early, because we've got to decorate this room tomorrow, and the rest of the house too."

She gave Karel a speaking glance and he responded manfully, observing that he was dog-tired himself, and how about them all making an early night of it. It did the trick; Cor allowed himself to be settled, and within ten minutes the room was quiet, with only the small table lamp with its dark shade to cast a comfortable glow on the ceiling. But Cor was still wide awake. Georgina undressed, put on her dressing gown and padded back to his bedside, a small plate piled with some of Mrs. Moggs' mince pies in her hand. She sat down on the side of his bed and offered him one. "They're delicious," she said. "I know Mrs. Stephens makes marvellous pastry too, but no two people ever make them the same." They munched together, while she regaled him with the day's small doings.

"Now tell me what you did," she suggested. He began in his turn, getting sleepier and sleepier, so that presently she was able to tuck him up, drop a kiss on his forehead, and go back to her room. She had begun to run the bath when she bethought herself of Beatrix. It was long past the child's bedtime, but the children were excited now that Christmas was so close. She picked up the mince pies once more and made her way to Beatrix's room. She wasn't asleep either, for Georgina could hear her rather shrill little voice talking. She knocked and said softly: "It's me—Georgina," and went inside. Beatrix was in bed; so were both the cats and Robby. The little girl rolled enormous blue eyes at her.

"George, I thought you would never come. We've all been so lonely." She caught sight of the plate in Georgina's hand. "What have you got there?"

Georgina told her, and went and sat on the bed, which made it rather crowded. She asked doubtfully, "Are these three going to stay the night?"

Beatrix bit into her pastry. "Oh, no. When Cousin

Julius comes in to tuck me up he'll take them downstairs. He doesn't mind—he calls them my nightlights." She smiled endearingly. "Their eyes shine in the dark, you know."

"Yes," agreed Georgina gravely, "I know. Will you go to sleep now? We've a lot to do in the morning—it'll be Christmas Eve."

She tucked Beatrix up, somewhat impeded by the sleeping animals, responded suitably to the little girl's hug, and returned to her room. It was very late by the time she got into her own bed. She lay awake listening for the sound of the Professor's car, but he still hadn't got home when she finally got to sleep.

When she reached the dining room the next morning, he was on the point of leaving. He wished her good morning briefly, adding mildly that it was just his bad luck to have work to do as early as nine o'clock in the morning.

"Very bad luck," said Georgina austerely. She hadn't slept well, and the knowledge that she wasn't looking her best did nothing to improve her feelings. She looked pointedly at the splendid room, with its bright fire and well appointed table, and then at the Professor's own large, immaculate person. Bad luck it might be, but it was nicely cushioned. She was preparing to voice her thoughts out loud when he said :

"No, don't say it. I can see by your face that you're about to tell me to give my money to the poor and go and work as a bus conductor and see how I should like that." He looked at the untidy mess he had made of his mail. "Be an angel, and sort out the letters while I get my coat, will you? I'm expecting something from Holland."

When he came back, coated and gloved, she handed him his letters. She would have liked to have said something—anything—to dispel his opinion of her, but there was a hard lump in her throat which made speech impossible, and anyway, what did it matter? She watched him go in silence, then turned to the remaining post. It reminded her that there had been a number of letters from Holland, several of them in a female handwriting. She sniffed dolefully, and if it hadn't been for Milly's appearance at that moment, would undoubtedly have burst into tears.

It was fortunate that there was so much to do that day, for there was no time to think. As soon as she had seen to Cor, they started to hang the decorations, and as everyone had their own ideas as to what looked best the results were unique and startling; only in the hall and drawing room did Dimphena and Georgina get their way. They had put their heads together days before, and now proceeded to fill the vases with charming arrangements of holly and Christmas roses and coloured baubles and the silvered pine cones they had collected on their walks. They twined holly and evergreens around the great fireplaces, and arranged the elaborate centrepiece they had all had a hand in on the dining table. There was a small tree for Cor's room, which they had put as close to him as possible, so that he could help with its decoration, and while they did that, Karel and Franz blew up the balloons which they insisted were an indispensable part of the decorations. Karel hung them in great colourful bunches all over the house—he hung the mistletoe as well, and then refused to tell them where. Luncheon was a merry meal, and when it was over, Georgina said:

"Now I'm going to the village—there are one or two last-minute things to get."

"I'll take you." Karel was eager.

She smiled at him. "I know you would, Karel, but have you forgotten the Sindings are coming over this afternoon?"

He pulled a face. "I'd forgotten." He turned to his sister. "I say, Phena, will they stay to tea?"

"Of course. But we'll have it early in the small sitting room, then we can have another tea in Cor's room after they've gone. If Julius comes home early, I daresay we could make our excuses." She looked at Georgina. "There's the tree to decorate—we usually do it before Julius comes home."

Georgina got up. "Wouldn't you have time to do it before your friends come?" She smiled at Franz.

"You'll sit with Cor, won't you, Franz, there's that marvellous jigsaw puzzle you started before lunch."

Having organised the afternoon, she lost no time in setting out for the village—it had stopped snowing, but there was plenty underfoot and it showed no signs of melting. She had put on her corduroy coat, leather boots, and the woolly tam with the pompom on top, then wrapped its matching scarf around her throat. The sun would soon be gone; it would be cold walking back. It was indeed early dusk when she left the village at length and started along the narrow, high-hedged lanes that led to Dalmers Place. It was cold now; cold enough to turn her breath into gossamer whorls around her head, and she could feel the first tingle of the night's frost through her gloves. The sky was clear; violet blue and spangled with stars. There would be a moon presently, but for a little while she would be a walking in the gathering dark. She went fast, swinging her basket and feeling suddenly festive. She had passed the last of the outlying cottages; there was nothing on the road; the only sound was that of her boots flattening the snow as she walked. She began to hum softly, then to whistle, and finally to sing. It seemed appropriate to choose something about winter snow, and she sang quite loudly, so that when the Rolls drew slowly to a halt beside her, she was surprised into standing still and staring at it. Its door opened and the Professor's quiet voice said, "Get in."

She felt remarkably foolish, standing there, cut off, as it were, in mid-song with the unexpectedness of it. She made no move at all, and he said again, "Get in."

"No, thank you," she uttered at last, remembering the au pair girl with devastating clarity. "I like to walk."

Professor Eyffert allowed a small sound to escape his lips.

"The fact that I disliked giving that au pair girl a lift seems to me to be a ridiculous reason for refusing my offer. That is the reason, isn't it?"

It was disconcerting to have her thoughts read so accurately. She handed him her basket without a word, and got in. They had travelled for perhaps half a minute before he broke the silence.

"Christmas shopping?" he asked.

It pleased her that her voice sounded normal. "No, not really. Just small things that are always forgotten until the last minute. We needed more tags and wrapping paper and Beatrix wanted some of those bullseyes they sell at the Post Office."

He changed gear. "Running errands in your free time, Nurse?"

She controlled her voice to sweet reasonableness. "I always go for a walk in the afternoons. Why should I not—run errands, as you say?"

"I'm only surprised to find you alone."

"There were people coming to tea—otherwise Karel and Dimphena would have come; Beatrix too."

He laughed. "We don't give you much time to yourself, between us. Do you mind?"

"Not in the least. I have only to say that I want to be on my own."

He brought the car to a gentle halt. "Do you want to be on your own now?" he queried blandly.

She glanced at his dim profile, wondering if he was serious. She wasn't sure. "No, thank you," she said meekly, playing safe.

"Good. Then I take it that we may hope for the pleasure of your company this evening for dinner—there will be a few friends—the children stay up."

"Thank you. But what about Cor?"

"He'll have an endless stream of visitors. I'll make sure that he's not lonely."

"He's very excited about Christmas—it's helped him to forget about his legs."

The Professor said quietly, "I think that it is you and not Christmas who have helped him to do that. I have to thank you for your unfailing kindness and devotion."

He swept the car between the gates and stopped at the little lodge. "I won't be a minute," he said, and was out of the car and up the narrow path to the little door, a package in his hand. Both Mr. and Mrs. Legg came to his knock; Georgina could hear them exchanging Christmas greetings and then the Professor's voice telling them to go indoors out of the cold. When he got back to the car, he handed a neatly wrapped box and said, "Hold it carefully, will you? It's Mrs. Legg's honey. We get a pot every Christmas and it's something very special."

He drove on through the trees to the house, where he said:

"Stay there a minute, will you? There's a great deal to take indoors." He went round to the boot and presently opened her door. "Do you mind taking a few things as you go?" The boot was full of parcels of every shape and size; he filled her arms with the smallest of them and said, "Go ahead, will you—Stephens will come out for the rest."

It was warm inside, and quiet, with a great fire burning steadily and the lamps casting little shadows on the white walls. She put her parcels tidily on one of the console tables and undid her coat. Outside she could hear the murmur of men's voices, and presently Stephens returned, followed by the Professor, who dropped an armful of packages into the nearest chair.

"Have they had tea yet, Stephens?" he enquired. His butler deposited half a dozen large boxes beside her own little pile.

"Ten minutes ago, sir. Milly shall bring up a fresh pot at once—unless you would like tea in your study?"

The Professor was staring at Georgina, who, aware of it, absorbed herself in the contemplation of a particularly fine arrangement of holly and gilded cones which she herself had thought up only that morning.

"No—no, thank you," he said absently, and then, "Very attractive."

"Yes, it is, isn't it?" agreed Georgina. She took a couple of steps towards the staircase, trying to think of some suitable way of taking her leave.

She stopped when he said, "You always wear uniform" in a tone of voice which suggested that he had explained something. "It's you who are attractive."

She went pink. "I wear uniform by your wish," she reminded him.

"Er—yes, that is so," he replied, very mild. "May I be allowed to forget that, just for this evening?" He smiled and her heart bounced against her ribs. "Will you not wear your prettiest dress?"

Georgina frowned. "And supposing I haven't got a pretty dress here?" she wanted to know, peevishly.

He looked taken aback, then looked at his watch. "I should have thought of that, shouldn't I? There's still plenty of time to run you up to St. Athel's to get whatever you want."

"It just so happens," said Georgina, still peevish, "that I have a dress here."

Her frown became thunderous when she saw the smile tugging the corners of his mouth. "What are you smiling about?" she demanded. He made no answer at all but walked over to her and kissed her, very lightly, upon one cheek. Thinking about it afterwards, which she did at great length, she was unable to describe it in any other terms than avuncular. Unsatisfactory, but true.

By the time she had put on the green dress and put the last careful pin into the complicated topknot of her hair, she was in a towering rage, although uncertain as to whether it was with herself or the Professor, and even more uncertain as to its cause. She put on the new velvet slippers, and with a last defiant spray of Rochas' *Femme*, over her well-turned-out person, went into Cor's room. That young gentleman let out an appreciative yell when he saw her—his spontaneous admiration doing much to soothe her ragged nerves. The dress, she was aware, did something for her; she hoped that it would strike Julius in the same light. If so, she would have no regrets about the price she had paid for it, not for the fact that she would be almost penniless until pay day.

She pirouetted before Cor and asked, "Will I do?"

He eyed her with the extravagant enthusiasm of a small boy.

"George, you're a smasher—cor love a duck!" he added, and cocked a questioning eye.

"I beg your pardon?" she said repressively. "And where did you learn that vulgar term?"

He looked innocent. "Vulgar? Mr. Legg often says it."

"I daresay. But does your guardian?"

"You mean Cousin Julius," he repeated patiently. "No. At least, I've not heard him."

"I should think not indeed! If you want to grow up like him you must try and speak as he does."

Cor wriggled. "But Cousin Julius has an accent; sometimes he sounds like a Dutchman."

Georgina looked severe. "That has nothing to do with it, and well you know it," to melt instantly when he said plaintively:

"My left knee hurts."

She was by him immediately, saying in a motherly voice, "Oh, dearest, you've wriggled and wriggled—you're worse than a worm!"

They giggled comfortably together while she took out the small pillow under the offending limb and smoothed it and put things to rights once more. She tidied his bed ruthlessly too, for, she said, "You will be having visitors—ever so many."

"Will you come and see me, George dear?"

She laughed a little and said gently, "Cor, how absurd you are! You see me every day and almost all day too—it'll be a nice change for you to see other people."

He nodded. "Yes, I know, but you don't always look like you do now. Please come, George."

She gave his bed a final pat. "All right, dear, I'll come. I won't be late anyway, because I want to go to church at seven in the morning, then I'll be back in time to watch you open your presents—that's if you can wait until then?"

"Rather, will you open your parcels too?"

"If I have any." He looked mysterious. "You'll get some, I expect."

He looked round as the door opened, and Beatrix,

very pleased with herself in a new cherry red dress, came in, followed by Dimphena in a pink velvet trouser suit and the pearl earrings, looking equally pleased. They stopped short inside the door and said in unison:

"George, you look gorgeous," and Dimphena went on, "You always look nice, but now you look...."

"Smashing," supplied Franz, and not to be outdone, Beatrix cried:

"No, she's beautiful!" and was echoed by Karel from the door.

"Just wait until Julius sets eyes on her; not a word, and of you. He will have a lovely surprise."

He looked at Georgina with admiration in his eyes, and made his way to where she was standing, produced a sprig of mistletoe from a pocket and kissed her. "Quite, quite beautiful," he said again, and she laughed, a little embarrassed but delighted too at their admiration.

"Go on with the lot of you!" she cried. "You'll turn me into a horrible conceited creature. I'm sure it's time we went down. Do go, all of you. I'll just fix Cor's table ready for his supper and slip down presently."

At the door Karel looked back, laughing. "Don't be long, you gorgeous girl—Julius will be speechless!"

She made some lighthearted reply, thinking that Julius had had six months in which to become speechless at the sight of her, without once giving any indication of doing any such thing; it was unlikely that he would be carried away by a pretty dress. She busied herself with Cor, wishing all at once that she wasn't going downstairs. It had been possible, so far, to maintain the cool friendly attitude towards the Professor which she felt he wished her to have—she had long ago worked out for herself that if he was considering marriage, the last thing he would want to do would be to give his future bride any cause for doubt or jealousy— he was that kind of a man, and because she loved him, she had striven to be exactly as he wanted. She remembered his kisses for a brief moment, and banished the thought. Men kissed girls for a variety of reasons; he could have been lonely, or happy, or unhappy, there

was no telling, and she had been the nearest female...
all the same, they were becoming good friends, despite
their squabbles; a little too good perhaps, and there
were still six weeks before she was due to go.

She sat Cor up before the tempting supper arranged
on his bedtable, stayed long enough to make sure that
he was going to eat it, and then went to the door, to
hesitate on its threshold and go to her room. She had
had an idea—a splendid one. She didn't stop to think
about it, but opened the small jewel case on the sofa
table, took out a rose diamond ring from its velvet box,
and put it on. It had been her mother's, and was a
perfect fit. She twisted it around her finger as she went
slowly along the corridor to the staircase, and just as
slowly down its broad steps, her left hand on the rail. A
few stairs from the bottom, she stopped, looking down
at the faces raised to her and feeling unexpectedly shy.
She looked uncertainly at Julius, standing a little apart
from the rest, and despite her resolution, her heart
skipped happily at the look on his face. It was Dimphena who cried, "George, I never knew you were
engaged—just fancy you being here all these weeks,
and none of us ever asked you!"

She watched the Professor's face go blank. He said
smoothly:

"Considering how delightful Miss Rodman looks, I
don't feel that we should be surprised." He looked at
her with a half-mocking smile. "My felicitations."

The others added their good wishes, and she wanted
to tell them that it wasn't true at all, and was on the
point of doing so, when he said:

"Shall we go into the drawing room and drink your
health before our guests arrive?" and somehow it
became impossible for her to speak, then there was no
more opportunity, for people started to arrive. She had
been stupidly impetuous again. Gregg was right, after
all. She might have a ring upon her finger, but she had,
in the heat of the moment, given no thought at all as to
her fiancé.

At dinner, she was glad to find that she was seated
between Mr. Sawbridge and a rather peppery old gentle-

man, who looked her over with a colicky eye and thanked heaven rather loudly that she wasn't one of those disgraceful young women who went about half naked. She surveyed him nonplussed, for it seemed an unpromising opening to conversation, but apparently he approved of her, and, when she asked cautiously if he had been in the army, embarked on a monologue of his life's history which lasted well into the roast goose. The little bouchées, filled with smoked salmon, which had preceded it had taken up very little of his attention, but she saw that the goose, handsomely accompanied by chestnuts and cranberry sauce, *haricots verts* and potatoes *noisettes*, was a dish worthy of his appetite. She turned to Mr. Sawbridge with some hesitation. She could not remember saying anything previously to him that had not been connected with bones, fractures, extensions or their like. It was a pleasant surprise to find that over and above these things, they had a great deal in common.

The goose was replaced with something delicious and frothy, which he assured her with a smile was called Zabaglione. It tasted of sherry, or possibly Madeira; she ate it up and hoped uneasily that it would mix with the claret and champagne.

There was coffee in the drawing room afterwards; the women admired the tree and gossiped about the parties they had been to. They made much of Beatrix, and were nice to Georgina. When the men joined them, her dinner partner made a beeline for her, and her heart warmed to him. She had been feeling a little lonely, due, she had no doubt, to the fact that Julius had not spoken to her since she had come downstairs. Her own silly fault, she admitted to herself, but it made no difference. She listened attentively to her companion, and watched the Professor at the other end of the room, looking handsome without any effort at all and paying marked attention to the eldest of the Sinding daughters, a tall willowy girl, with a face like a well-bred horse. Georgina had disliked her before, now she hated her. It was fortunate for her peace of mind that Stephens came in at that moment with the punch bowl, which was the signal for Beatrix to go to bed. She kissed her guardian good night, and made polite adieux to the guests, leaving Georgina till last.

"Are you coming with me?" she whispered. Georgina stood up, aware that the Professor was watching her as she made her excuses to the old gentleman. She took Beatrix's hand, smiled uncertainly at Julius across the room, and slipped out of the room. They went at once to Cor, who was already sleepy from an extra large supper and a superfluity of visitors. All the same, he had to be told every small thing which had occurred, together with an account of what everyone wore and ate.

"Cousin Julius said the party was going like a bomb," he confided. "He came up when they left the dining room—he said there was a galaxy of lovely ladies, George. What's a galaxy?"

She answered absently. She wouldn't go back to the drawing room. No one would be likely to miss her, except perhaps the peppery old gentleman.

"You look sad," said Beatrix. "You oughtn't to, George, because you were by far the prettiest lady there."

Georgina smiled rather ruefully at her small admirer. "No, darling, not really. Though it's sweet of you to think so. Now who's for bed? You first, poppet, then I'll come and tuck Cor up, and go to bed too."

While she was helping Beatrix, that small damsel asked sapiently, "Why aren't you going back to the party, George? Don't you like the people?"

"Oh, rather," said Georgina, falsely cheerful. "But they'll be going home soon and I want to be up early in the morning—it was a lovely party," she added for good measure. It seemed to satisfy Beatrix, anyway, for she climbed into bed, closed her eyes, and declared her intention of going to sleep at once. Georgina said comfortably, "That's right, darling, the quicker you go to sleep, the quicker Father Christmas will come. Ginger and Toto are tired too."

She indicated the slumbering animals, returned Beatrix's hug, and went back to Cor. He was ready for bed too. She prepared him for the night, tucked him up, and went to her own room, where she sat down in one of the little buttoned chairs and listened to the faint sounds of the party, deep in thought and from time to time contemplating the ring on her finger. Presently, she sighed and took it off, went to the cupboard and got out the Professor's football socks which Milly had unearthed from somewhere, and began to fill them with the little presents she had collected for the two children. They would have their big presents after breakfast, but Dimphena had told her when she had asked that the two little ones always had a sock as well, and had agreed readily to Georgina seeing to them. She glanced at the clock when she had finished, astonished to find that it was so late. The party was breaking up; she could hear distant farewells and the crunch of car tyres in the snow. She walked softly along the corridor, the well-filled socks clasped to her green velvet bodice. She was half way down the little passage leading to Beatrix's room when she heard someone come upstairs, and turned to see the Professor, with Robby at his heels, coming towards her. She lifted a warning finger and whispered "Hush!", whereupon he took her by the arm, opened his bedroom door, and drew her inside.

"Where the devil did you get those socks?" he wanted to know in an interested voice. "I haven't seen them since I was at Cambridge."

She had expected him to say something quite different; she wasn't sure what, but certainly nothing as prosaic as a query about socks. She said quickly, "Oh dear, do you mind? I asked Milly for some old ones—they're large, you see," she explained, "but I can easily find something else."

He was leaning against the tallboy, with his hands in his pockets. She envied him his ease of manner.

"Why should I mind? I'm glad I can contribute in some small way to your splendid efforts." He smiled lazily at her and she was aware that he was concealing amusement. He went on gently, "You didn't come back to the party."

She said cautiously, "No. By the time the children were tucked up...."

"Two hours ago." His bright gaze flickered over her. "You look charming." He shifted his weight from one long leg to the other. "Damsel in green," he murmured.

Georgina gave him a suspicious look. No one had called her a damsel before. "I've got some in the cellar," he went on surprisingly. "It's a Dutch liqueur—the names's seventeenth-century...."

She said shyly, "Oh, for one minute I thought you meant me."

"I do. You're a damsel, aren't you? And you're in green... and just as heady as the liqueur...." He broke off as there was a gentle tap on the door, and said without surprise, "Come in, Karel."

Just as his cousin had said, Karel exclaimed "Good lord, Julius's football socks! Where did you get those?"

She repeated herself patiently. "Milly found them."

He nodded. "Good old Milly—always knows where everything is. Are the kids asleep?"

It was Julius who answered him. "I imagine so. Georgina hushed me severely when I came upstairs... in my own house too!"

She said contritely, "I'm sorry—I was just going in with this." She indicated the unwieldy socks.

The Professor straightened himself. "That's all right, we'll all go." He opened a drawer in a chest. "Here, my dear girl, stuff these in as well."

She did as she was told, beginning to enjoy herself. Beatrix was asleep, her small pink mouth slightly open, her hair all over the pillow. The cats watched without moving while the sock was tied to the bedpost, not even stirring when Robby padded in silently and blew gently over them. Cor was asleep too, and stayed asleep even while the Professor tied his sock within an inch or so of his head, so that he could reach it on waking.

When they were all in the corridor again, Georgina said: "Well, good night." But the Professor fixed her with a blue eye which held a gleam in its depths. "You're coming downstairs for a drink." He spoke positively and when she started to protest, put up a large hand.

"No excuse. Even if I have to carry you—if you're not too heavy."

It would have been useless to argue. She walked between them, and when they reached the hall, Julius said:

"Go along to Stephens, will you, Karel—tell him to fetch up that bottle of Damsel in Green, and bring it back with you. I'm going to open it in honour of our own Damsel in Green."

She was half way across the hall when he caught up with her, and stopped her with a big hand on her arm; it sent a tremble up her arm and she moved a little away from him. "I'm not in the least heavy," she said.

He chuckled. "Did that rankle? I can tease too, Georgina."

She repeated in a silly way, "Tease too?"

He nodded. "Were you not teasing us this evening?" he asked blandly. "I did not think so at the time, but now I am sure that you were."

He caught her hand and held it up, once more ringless, and she looked up at him, trying to read his face. Her splendid plan had gone sadly wrong. She fought a desire to burst into tears, and bit her lip to stop its trembling. He said very gently, "I imagine you had a very good reason."

She nodded, and he went on, ignoring the lip, "Well, I'm glad it was a tease, because Karel has had a face as long as a fiddle."

He broke off as that young gentleman joined them and she stood beside them, listening to the Professor dealing with the whole regrettable episode with a masterly, light-hearted touch which gave her no blame, and turned the whole thing into a joke. A less scrupulous girl might have derived satisfaction from the look on Karel's face, but she did not even see it, for she was still trying to understand the expression on Julius's face.

It was one o'clock before she went to bed; they had sat around the fire with Dimphena and Franz, talking. The Professor had been friendly, slightly withdrawn, and, she feared, totally unmoved by the new dress, despite his polite remarks. She was just dropping off to sleep when it struck her forcibly that her thoughts were in direct contradiction to her resolves.

It was cold when she left the house the next morning and made her way to the garage. She was in the Mini and had just switched on the ignition when Julius said out of the darkness, "Good morning, Miss Rodman, and a Happy Christmas. Move over—if we are to risk life and limb on these appalling lanes, I might as well be responsible for the damage."

She moved over without a word, her heart beating a rapid tattoo which she felt sure he could hear. It seemed not; he got in beside her and shut the door with the air of a man fitting himself into a too tight coat. It was a good thing that she was a normal-sized girl; as it was, it would be impossible for them to be any closer.

"You're quiet," he observed. "Did I startle you?"

She lied in haste, "Not in the least." and held her breath when he went on, "Then why are you so breathless?"

He spoke with the air of a man who expects an answer, and she answered hurriedly, "Well, perhaps I was a little," and remembered to say good morning and Happy Christmas in her turn.

"That's better." He didn't speak again, but eased the little car down the drive and into the lane. They skidded several times on the way to the village, but she was so happy to be with him that she hardly noticed.

The little church was full, its early morning chill scented with holly and chrysanthemums; Georgina enjoyed the service and said so on the way home. Her companion grunted an agreement and then made no further contribution to the conversation. She became aware of this in mid-sentence, and asked:

"Would you rather I didn't talk? Does it make you nervous?" and was taken aback by the gust of laughter which shook him, and then affronted when he said smoothly:

"Not at all—I enjoy your chatter." Which remark most effectively put a stop to her uttering another word.

He brought the Mini to a halt before the door and got out to go round to help her over the snow. It was still very dark, but there were lights at some of the windows of the rambling old house, and the clear frosty sky made the stars seem very close. Georgina, her head thrown back, stood gazing upwards. "I do like Christmas—it's a wonderful time."

She felt his hand tighten on her arm. "Full of the Christmas spirit, I hope, Miss Rodman."

She brought her gaze down from the sky to the level of his face above hers. "You mean loving and giving?" she asked, simply, like a child.

He said slowly, "Yes, that's what I mean—loving and giving." He loosened his hold on her arm and added matter-of-factly, "Look out for the steps, they're slippery."

The day promised to be a wholly happy one. Contrary to custom, and as a concession to Cor's legs, they all took their presents to open in his room. It took a considerable time for everyone to examine their gifts, exclaim over them and thank the givers. Eventually they went away to get ready for church, except Georgina, who declared her intention of at least making Cor's bed, if nothing else. She went around the room while he unwillingly washed his hands and face, and collected the gay wrapping papers and ribbons with which it was strewn. Her own presents she carried to her own room; they made quite a large pile, for they had all given her something, from Beatrix's lop-sided pincushion to the Professor's silver Valentine mirror, an exquisite trifle which must have cost a pretty penny, although she had long ago come to the conclusion that he didn't have to worry about pennies, nor, for that matter, pounds either.

They ate their dinner in Cor's room. With almost no fuss at all, a table was brought in, erected and laid and decorated with crackers, holly and paper streamers, and Cor was left in happy contemplation of it while they went away to dress. Georgina put on the green dress once more, and returned to Cor's room to find the Professor already there, discussing the merits of the bicycle he had given him. However, they abandoned this interesting topic as soon as she joined them and Julius went to pour her a drink, leaving her by Cor's bed, wondering why there were traces of tears on the little boy's cheeks. But by the time they had eaten their turkey with all its delicious trimmings, and sampled the Christmas pudding, and rounded all this off with another glass of Damsel in Green, there was no sign of unhappiness in Cor's face. She decided it was probably some small argument, which, naturally enough, his guardian had won.

The cause of his tears was only made apparent to her at the end of the evening. They were dispersing to their various rooms when the Professor remarked casually that they would all be going to Holland within the next day or so. Cor would, of course, have to stay behind, and naturally enough, she was to stay with him.

Much later, in bed, she went over their brief conversation about it, if the few words they exchanged could be so described. After a little while she blew her nose with unnecessary vigour, reminded herself that it had been one of the best Christmases she had ever known, and went determinedly to sleep, with the tears she hadn't bothered to wipe away still wet on her cheeks.

CHAPTER 8

GEORGINA saw the Professor for only a brief moment before they went away; it seemed even briefer by virtue of his manner, which was business-like in the extreme. She was told in a few crisp sentences about X-rays, Mr. Sawbridge's expected visit and the radiographer, and finally, the physiotherapist. She was also to expect a telephone call from Holland each evening between five and six o'clock. In the event of an emergency she was to telephone him at any time of the day or night— Stephens would give her the number.

He had sent for her during the quiet oasis of time between tea and dinner. She had heard the car a little earlier, and then his steps on the staircase, but contrary to usual custom, he had passed Cor's door without entering, and it was very nearly dinner time when Milly came to ask her to go down to the study. Georgina, who had been playing cards with the two children, and in the heat of the game had cast off her cap, ran downstairs, ramming it upon her rather untidy hair, to arrive slightly out of breath before the Professor. He was resplendent in white tie and tails and obviously on his way to some social function, and equally obviously, in haste to be gone. She listened carefully to what he had to say, then in a cool little voice which disguised her unhappiness, assured him that she would take good care of Cornelis and carry out his instructions, and then added a rider to the effect that she hoped that they would enjoy their holiday. Then she stood mute, for she could think of nothing else to say, and nor, it seemed, could he, for a moment of staring at her, he wished her a civil goodbye in a rather absent-minded manner, as though his mind was already busy with other matters. She went back upstairs slowly; in six weeks' time she would most probably be back in hospital, and her stay at Dalmers Place would be a thing of the past. She began, deliberately, to think about her future at St. Athel's.

The house was quiet when they had gone. Georgina, doing morning chores for Cor, looked at his pale face and guessed at the disappointment behind his deadpan expression. She decided against her usual afternoon walk, and instead read *The Wind in the Willows* until she was hoarse, then after tea sat down at the piano. She wasn't an accomplished pianist, but she had a good ear for a tune, and a natural gift for making a melody come alive. She meandered through snatches of Gilbert and Sullivan, the latest pop, a good deal of *West Side Story*, and ended with Handel's *Water Music*. She hadn't realised that Cor's voice was so angelic—it soared effortlessly in accompaniment, and presently she joined him, to the pleasure of them both. They might have gone on a good deal longer, but the ringing of the telephone put a stop to it, for it was no hasty three-minute call which the Professor made, but a lengthy, comfortable chat. She pictured him, sitting at ease in his Dutch home, while Cor chattered away happily in a Dutch she couldn't hope to understand. Every now and then he would roar with laughter, and she found herself wondering what it was about Julius that could so enchant his small ward, even from several hundred miles away. It was a silly question, anyway, she told herself as she got up and went to her room; she was only too well aware how hopelessly and help-lessly she herself had succumbed to that same enchant-ment. She busied herself gathering together the mater-ials for the making of the rag doll she had promised Beatrix, and went back to Cor, hoping that there might be a message for her. There was not. She sat down by the fire and listened patiently to Cor's excited account of the arrival in Holland. "Beatrix was sick," he stated dramatically, "and there's ice on the pond—perhaps they'll skate...." The corners of his mouth turned down and she made haste to ask, "A pond? In your guardian's garden? I didn't know. Do tell."

"It's big," he said importantly, "and the garden's

bigger than this one—but the house is quite different—it's square and the windows are large."

"Will you draw it for me?" she suggested, happy to find something that would keep him cheerfully occupied until his supper time. He drew the exterior, and much encouraged by her praise, a plan of the house. It looked rather fine, she thought, if Cor's draughtsmanship was to be believed.

"Has it a name?" she wanted to know.

He nodded. "Bergenstijn." He made her repeat it after him until she had it right, then described exactly where it was. "Near the Queen's palace, George dear, and there are a lot of trees round it, and little green fields, and if you go up a narrow road at the side you come to Princess Beatrix's house, though we never do, of course." He chattered on until his supper arrived and she went to her own lonely meal. It was while she was tucking him up for the night that he said:

"Cousin Julius didn't like leaving me behind, but he explained that my aunts and uncles and cousins who go to Bergenstijn each New Year might be disappointed if they didn't go as usual, and they wanted to see Dimphena and Franz and Beatrix, even if they couldn't see me. He said it wouldn't be kind or polite, but he asked my advice about it, and if I didn't want them to go, he could always telephone and say they wouldn't be able to manage it...of course I said I didn't mind staying a bit if you were here too." He puffed out his chest and said with childish dignity, "Julius said I was a chip off the old block and he had known all along he could count on me."

Georgina turned back the bedclothes. She said, "Golly, I bet he feels proud of you."

Cor looked pleased. "Yes. Do you know what he said about you?"

She was massaging a leg; her hand did not falter although her heart gave a lurch. "No—and I don't think that your guardian would expect you to repeat it to me," she said repressively.

"You always say 'your guardian' and not Julius. Why?"

She started on the other leg. "Your guardian employs me. It would be rude of me to call him anything else."

"He calls you Miss Rodman and we all call you George." He was silent for a moment, then blurted out: "I don't like that—nor does Beatrix—she said so. Don't you like each other? Karel kissed you under the mistletoe, but Cousin Julius didn't."

Georgina bit her lip. "Darling, of course we like each other." She paused. It would be better if she ignored the last part of his remark. "Look, I tell you what I'll do—I'll call him Julius while we're keeping house together, shall I? Just to you."

Cor brightened. "Yes, please, George dear, and I'm sure he won't mind, because he told me to do exactly as you said and to take great care of you because there aren't any more like you. What do you suppose he meant?" He looked at her. "You've gone very red in the face—is it hard work doing my legs?"

"Yes. I don't think Julius meant anything much; only that nurses are scarce, you know, and hard to come by. There, no more for tonight. I'm going to tuck you up and then go and telephone my aunt, and mind you're asleep when I come upstairs."

She kissed him goodnight and gave him a hug and said cheerfully:

"We'll make a calendar tomorrow—you know, little squares, one for each day; then we can cross them off every evening—the days go fast that way."

Actually, the days did go fast. There was the visit of the radiographer and his technician to X-ray Cor's legs; they came in the morning and had coffee and explained their complicated machine to Cor, so that when his guardian telephoned that evening, the conversation was highly technical. Mr. Sawbridge came too, a day or two later, and pronounced himself very satisfied with the results of the X-rays. He did a great deal of adjusting of the traction and explained at some length to Cor about the necessity of walking carefully with gutter crutches once he was on his feet. "I've seen that marvellous bike Julius gave you for Christmas," he said. "No getting on to it until I say so." He sat down on the bed, abruptly shedding his professional manners. "Let's hear what they're up to in Holland."

Georgina left them together, whistled to Robby, and went into the garden. Mr. Sawbridge stayed to lunch, and harped for an unnecessarily long time upon her future career in hospital. He looked at her speculatively and said gently, "You will make an excellent Sister, George—that is, of course, if that's what you wish to be."

She didn't answer him, because to say "No, I'd rather marry Julius" would probably have shocked him profoundly, and she liked him far too much to put him out in any way.

It was New Year's Eve, and the evening telephone conversation took so long that she deduced that the entire family were taking it in turns to have a word with Cor. It was therefore surprising when he said:

"George, Julius wants to speak to you."

She took the telephone from him and sat down composedly on the side of his bed, her orderly mind already busy with a report. The Professor's voice said in her ear, "No, I don't want a report—I had a word with Sawbones. How are you?"

She said, breathless, "Very well, thank you," and waited.

He said to surprise her, "I shall think of you at midnight."

She could think of nothing to say but "Why?" and heard him laugh.

"Wanting an answer again, Georgina? You will have to wait for this one. In the meantime, goodnight."

She answered mechanically, feeling disappointed. He hadn't even bothered to wish her a Happy New Year.

She hadn't intended to sit up to see the New Year in, there seemed little point in it. She had telephoned Aunt Polly earlier in the evening, there was really nothing more to do except finish the rag doll, and when that was done, get ready for bed. Her movements got slower and slower; she discovered numberless small tasks that needed doing before she could turn out the light. Finally she took a book and went and sat by the fire in Cor's room; he was sound asleep, but he was company.

The clock in her bedroom chimed midnight, and she put down the book which she hadn't been reading anyway. She wondered what Julius was doing—Cor had said that all the family would be there—and friends too—smart, sophisticated women with marvellous hair-dos and couture dresses. She closed her eyes on tears, then opened them as the telephone rang just once. She looked at Cor as she lifted the receiver, but he hadn't stirred. She said softly "Yes?"

"You stayed up," said the Professor's voice, equally softly. "A Happy New Year to you, my Damsel in Green."

She smiled at the receiver. "Oh, thank you. And I hope you have a wonderful year."

"Don't worry—I shall. Don't go away, here are the others."

They spoke to her in turn, Dimphena and Karel and Franz, and last of all Beatrix, very sleepy, and after her, the Professor again.

"Now go to bed," he said. "Goodnight."

She did as he had said, and lay awake for quite a while, wondering why he had telephoned. It would be lovely to think that he had missed her, but common sense urged her to discard this delightful idea. The Dutch made a lot of New Year—probably he had telephoned the Stephens and Milly too. She went to sleep telling herself that this was more than likely, and in the morning was bitterly disappointed to discover that this was exactly what he had done.

There was a letter from one of her friends at St. Athel's in the morning's post. Amongst a great deal of hospital gossip, the writer informed her that the grapevine had it that dear George was to be offered Cas: when Sister left in March, although, continued the writer, George had probably got her future nicely settled for herself; that same grapevine having also supplied her friend with the news that Professor Eyffert was a bachelor, and a very eligible one. This remark was embellished with a maximum of asterisks, question marks and exclamations, and accompanied by a plea for inside information.

Georgina read it through to the end. Three months earlier, she would have been overjoyed about Cas.—now it really didn't seem to matter, although she knew already that she would accept the post if it were offered; indeed, she had little choice if she wanted to pave the way to a successful career. She tore the letter up into small pieces, and went to blanket-bath Cor.

The physiotherapist came after lunch and offered to stay for an hour after she had given Cor his treatment, so that Georgina was able to walk to the village and do some shopping. The weather had changed; the snow had turned to slush and the wind blew fiercely into her face as she battled her way back to Dalmers Place. It had been nice to get out though—when the others returned she would be able to make up for the days she had spent indoors. The physiotherapist stayed to tea; she was a middle-aged woman with children of her own and a great favourite with Cor; they were both sorry to see her go.

The wind grew stronger as the evening advanced, whining and howling around the house so that the old building was full of small sounds. When Georgina came back after her dinner, it was to find Cornelis sitting stiffly in his bed, listening. She gave him a keen glance, and asked, "What's up?"

"It's the wind, it makes such a noise."

She went over to the fire and poked it to a blaze. "I like it," she observed, not quite truthfully, "especially when we're so cosy here. Shall I tell you a story?"

He relaxed. "Yes, please—will you come and sit here, by me?" He pushed his bedtable aside, a little petulant. "Cousin Julius said it was raining at Bergenstijn—he said the house was full of people getting on each other's nerves." They laughed together. "They're all going to the theatre in Amsterdam tomorrow," he added, not laughing any more.

"Very nice too," she said bracingly. "When you get back on those legs of yours, I thought we might go to the pantomime—Beatrix too, of course. Just we three. Would you like that?"

He relaxed still further. "Yes, please." He made

room for her on the edge of the bed and she began a story about a dog and a cat and a donkey, which became so involved that it was obvious to them both that it would need several successive nights to bring it to a conclusion.

The bad weather continued for several days, but now that Mr. Coppin had started Cor's lessons again, she was able to get out each morning. Robby ambled along with her, getting very wet so that it took her several minutes to dry him when they got back home; but he was excellent company and worth the trouble. Mr. Sawbridge came again, expressed satisfaction at his handiwork and ordered gentle exercises, and spoke, with professional caution, of the traction coming down in four weeks—a piece of news heralded with delight by Cor and shared by Georgina, although her pleasure was tempered with dismay. Four weeks would go quickly; by the time the Professor was back from Holland, it would be three weeks, and in those three weeks she couldn't hope to see him every day. Mr. Sawbridge stayed to luncheon too, during which he substantiated the news from the grapevine.

"A splendid opportunity for you, George," he observed. "Do you intend to make Casualty your career?"

She looked at her plate. "Yes, I suppose so," she replied without enthusiasm, and caught his sharp glance. "It—it was a surprise," she said lamely. "I can't quite believe it. I know I'm very lucky."

"Lucky?" he said surprisingly. "Only if that is what you want."

She didn't answer that, and after a moment he began to talk about Bergenstijn. It seemed that he had been on holiday there and had a fondness for it.

Contrary to her expectations, the week went quickly, although the last day dragged, partly due to the fact that Cor had wakened earlier than usual and had insisted on starting his day at least an hour earlier than was his wont, so that by the time the travellers were expected, he was already tired and slightly peevish. Matters got worse as time passed and they didn't arrive; it was in vain that Georgina pointed out that the weather was bad enough to delay the plane, and even if it had arrived on time, the Professor wasn't likely to tear through the country at seventy miles an hour in that same weather. As if to add strength to her argument, the rain drummed against the window panes, and as if that wasn't enough there was a lightning flash, followed by a crashing roll of thunder that sent the three animals under the bed and changed Cor's ill-humour to a fright he strove to hide. Georgina, who disliked storms herself, drew her chair nearer to the bed and was relieved when Stephens came in and asked in a fatherly fashion if there was anything they wanted and remarked in his calm, rather flat voice that in his opinion the storm, although violent, would soon pass. Doubtless the travellers would be delayed, and in the meantime, should they need him, he would be close at hand. He went quietly away again, leaving an aura of secure comfort behind him.

"How about finishing that story?" asked Georgina. She settled on the bed beside her patient and put an arm round his thin shoulders, and was soon deep in the improbable adventures of the dog, the cat and the donkey. So deep, in fact, that they barely heard the wind and the rain, or the occasional bellowing of the thunder; it was Robby, coming out from under the bed and making for the door, which caused them to look round.

Beatrix came in first and hurled herself at them, with Dimphena and Franz close behind. Georgina was hugged and embraced, and when Karel appeared, kissed too, very heartily—he still had an arm around her when the Professor walked in. His glanced flickered over them both, then he smiled and said, "Hallo there, Nurse. Did you think we were never coming?" and not waiting for an answer, went over to Cor's bed, where he stayed for ten minutes or more before going away again, having first admonished everyone to be ready for dinner within half an hour. His remark reminded Georgina that Cor should have his supper too, and after promising to return before he was put to bed, the rest of them went away too, leaving her to calm down a very excited small boy.

Dinner was gay, with everyone bent on telling Georgina everything that had happened in the past fourteen days in the shortest possible time—everyone, that was, but the Professor, who, although he joined in the talk, was thoughtful. Georgina peeped at him once or twice, and each time found his eyes fixed steadily on her, so that she was unable to prevent herself from putting up a questing hand to make sure that her cap was sitting at its proper angle upon her head. It was, and she frowned a little—surely her hair wasn't coming down? she waited a minute, then put her hand up again, to arrest it in mid-air when he said softly, "Not a hair out of place, Miss Rodman." She flushed and avoided his eye until the end of the meal when he asked Stephens to take his coffee to his study, and said, as they crossed the hall, "Perhaps you will be good enough to come and see me when you have had coffee, Miss Rodman."

He was standing with his back to the fire when she went in. He waved a hand towards a chair drawn up to its warmth and said, "Sit down, won't you? Did you find it very tedious, alone with Cor?"

She looked shocked. "Good gracious, no. We haven't had a dull minute, Cor and I. And even if I had found it tedious, it's my job."

He stared at her from under lowered lids. "You're frank. And is that how you regard your stay here—as a job?"

"Oh no. You see, I'm very fond of Cor and Beatrix—and Franz and Dimphena...."

"You forget Karel."

"Karel? Oh, yes. They're like brothers and sisters."

She saw the look on his face, a look she had never seen before.

"Is that how you regard them?" he wanted to know.

She met his bright gaze. "I'm sorry, Professor. I didn't mean to be impertinent—my wretched tongue!" She got to her feet. "Please will you forget that I said that?"

He said coolly, "No. Why should I? I don't find it impertinent, merely illuminating." He smiled at her and she caught her breath. "Now sit down again and tell me about Cor."

She sat, regained her composure and answered his questions with her usual calm directness. When she had finished, he said:

"About a month, Old Sawbones thinks. He won't commit himself, of course." He left the fire and sat down opposite her. "He tells me that you are to be offered a Sister's post. Casualty, I presume. You're pleased?"

She looked down at her hands, folded tidily in her lap. "Yes," she said baldly.

"There is something else you would rather do with you life, perhaps?"

She examined her nails—well shaped pink nails on her capable hands.

"I expect we would all rather do something else. . . ." she remembered to whom she was speaking, and said in a flurry, "Of course I'm delighted—it's a wonderful opportunity." She got up for the second time. "If there's nothing further, Professor, I told Cor I'd be up soon after dinner."

He got up too. "Thank you for taking care of him while we were away. I wouldn't have left him with anyone else. You took your days off?"

She was at the door. "Well, no. . . ." and stood still waiting for his cool annoyance.

"I imagined you didn't," was all he said. "That means three days, does it not? Supposing you go the day after tomorrow?"

He had followed her to the door and opened it for her, and then took his hand from it and caught her by the shoulder and kissed her without haste. When he finally let her go, she stared at him, speechless. She still hadn't found her tongue when he remarked, to puzzle her for the rest of a wakeful night:

"Your uniform isn't enough." He sounded resigned.

She didn't see him until the following evening, when he was as politely friendly as Mr. Sawbridge might have been. And the next day she went home.

She took the Mini, driving rather recklessly through

the grey, wet countryside. The cottage was snug and bright with winter flowers; the little hall smelled of furniture polish and an occasional whiff of something savoury in the kitchen. She was welcomed with delight and love by the two old ladies. She looked at their kind, wise faces, and longed to pour out her heart to them; instead, she hugged them extravagantly and went out to the car to fetch her case. There was a wildly outsize box of chocolates from Holland too, and an armful of spring flowers Legg had wordlessly handed to her—and a box she didn't remember putting in the car. She carried it indoors, and they opened it in the little sitting room, in front of the fire. There were two bottles of claret inside and a letter to Aunt Polly, addressed to her in the Professor's crabbed scribble. Georgina gave it to her aunt without comment and went to take off her coat. When she got back, Mrs Mogg had brought in the coffee and there was no sign of the letter, nor did Aunt Polly mention it.

There was a great deal to talk about anyway— among them the rumour that she might get a Sister's post sooner than she had expected. She did her best to be enthusiastic about this, harping at length about the bigger salary and not having to be on duty until eight o'clock each morning, but somehow the conversation got around to Dalmers Place, and she found herself relating all the small day-to-day incidents with an increasing enthusiasm and pleasure; when at length she paused, Aunt Polly said, "You're going to find hospital life very different from Dalmers Place. Three months is a long time. . . ." and then without any warning at all, "Did Professor Eyffert say anything to you about his getting married, dear?"

Georgina got up and went to the window and straightened a curtain that needed nothing done to it at all. "Yes, he did. But that was all—I mean, he didn't say who to, or when. He—he said it would be best for the children. He told me once that he was lonely."

She wandered back and sat down by the fire again, thinking of him eating his breakfast alone in an untidy flurry of letters and newspapers. Presumably his wife would keep him company. She hoped so.

"An Englishwoman?" hazarded her aunt gently. "Not, I hope, one of those Sinding girls."

"I don't think so. They've been over several times, but. . . ." she left the sentence unfinished. If he was in love with one of them, he had concealed it very effectively, and as there was no point in doing that, it couldn't be them. "There's someone called Madame LeFabre in Holland, I suppose. The children have mentioned her. Julius goes to Holland frequently."

She hadn't noticed that she had called him Julius, and her aunt said nothing.

The next day the weather cleared a little, and Georgina, in old jeans and still older sweater, went down the garden to the potato clamp. She had her basket of potatoes, and was picking sprouts, when Mrs Mogg called from the back door. Georgina got up off her knees and shouted:

"Oh, Moggy, is it important?"

"Not for me, it's not," said the worthy Mrs Mogg. "It's the gentleman from Dalmers Place."

Georgina stood where she was. Her first thought was of pure joy, her second of rage that he should come unheralded when she was looking just about as unattractive as possible. Perhaps if she could sneak in quietly, she could run upstairs and put on a dress. . . . She picked up her basket and tore down the narrow brick path. Karel was standing at the back door, waiting for her. She checked her headlong flight when she saw him, and composed her face into a welcoming smile. How silly of her to have imagined for one minute that it was Julius who had called!

She said gaily, "Hallo, Karel. How nice to see you," and he caught hold of her basket, dropped a light kiss on her cheek, and said, "Yes, isn't it?" and gave her a searching look, so that she looked away quickly and busied herself kicking off her rubber boots.

"Dressed to kill, aren't you?" he observed cheerfully, as she led the way indoors.

She sketched a brief curtsy. "Careful, Karel, compliments like that go to my head. Come and see Aunt Polly and I'll get coffee."

He was going back to Cambridge the next day; without quite knowing how it had happened, she found herself changing into a tweed suit and a rather dashing little hat, preparatory to going out to lunch with him. They went to the Grapevine at Cavendish, where they ate, among other things, lobster Thermidor. Over the rum omelette she chose to follow it, she said with an unconscious wistfulness:

"I shall never get used to eating hospital food again. This sort of thing—" she waved an expressive hand over the table—"and the gorgeous meals at Dalmers Place. . . . I used to think how wonderful it would be if someone took me to some place where I could order what I liked, now I've had three months of that kind of living, and it's spoilt me for sausages and roast lamb."

"Don't try to make me believe that no one ever takes you out."

"Don't be silly, of course I go out. But housemen don't have much money, I wouldn't be so mean as to insist on all the most expensive places."

"Tell you what," Karel said kindly, "I'll come down to town and take you out once in a while. Anyway, old Julius is sure to ask you down to Dalmers Place. I'll tell him to lay on something special—caviare, and—er— saddle of hare and a crême brulée made with at least a dozen eggs."

"Don't you dare," she said heatedly. "Don't you dare to ask him to invite me. . . . I wouldn't come anyway."

Her companion looked amazed. "Why ever not? The kids will want to see you, anyway."

"Yes, I know—I'm going to miss them terribly, but once my job is over I'd rather not go back to Dalmers Place."

His gaze was disconcerting. "Have you hated it so much, Georgina?"

She felt near to tears; she hadn't meant it to sound like that at all. "Oh, Karel, no! I've loved every minute of it. I shall hate going; I can't even bear to think about it." She stopped. As usual her rebel tongue was having its own way. "I mean that, truly I do—I've been so happy, Karel."

She looked at him beseechingly and tried again. "You see, my sort of life isn't your sort of life."

"That's a damn silly thing to say. If Julius knew...."

She went red and then white. "Karel, please don't ever tell him. Promise—you must promise!"

He gave her a discerning look, smiled suddenly and said reassuringly, "I promise, Georgina. Cross my heart."

She let out a relieved sigh and said with an effort, "What a silly conversation! Let's forget it."

"O.K. Can't help, I suppose, old lady?"

She was touched. She shook her head. "You're almost the nicest person I know, Karel."

"Almost? There lies the crux of the matter, eh? All right, I won't say another word," and he plunged into a wildly improbable story about life at Cambridge.

He took her back home in time for tea, and left after, with a casual "See you soon," and a brotherly hug which gave her the shoulder-ache for hours after. As the Morgan roared down the lane, Aunt Polly murmured:

"Such a nice young man, Georgina." She sighed and went on briskly, "Ask Mrs. Mogg to open the claret, will you, dear? We can all do with a glass, I fancy."

Georgina had a wild welcome from Cor and Beatrix when she got back—almost, she observed laughingly, as though she had been away for three weeks instead of only three days. She had a welcome from the Professor too—a hurried one as they passed each other in the hall. He, it seemed, was on his way up to London—St. Athel's had some dire emergency, and he was doubtful if he would be back before midnight. She thought he looked pale and rather cross, and the smile she offered him was not returned.

He wasn't home the next day either, she went through the day's routine, very aware that the month had shrunk to less than three weeks and there was nothing she could do about it. Illogically, she was disappointed to find that the friendship which had grown between them had come to its apparent end. There were no more mornings helping him with his post; no more reports given in the study after dinner, and only very rarely did he get home in time to have tea with the rest of them. He was as charmingly polite and kind as he always had been, only there was a barrier between them—a withdrawal on his part, which, being feminine, she naturally put down to feminine influence other than her own. Each day slid into the next, each one a little quicker than the last, until the day Mr. Sawbridge came to look at Cor's legs, and stated positively that he would be down to remove the traction in five days' time. Georgina accompanied him to the door, and he said, "Well, George, back to St. Athel's in a week or so. I daresay they'll manage once Cor's got used to his legs again, and that won't take long."

She agreed in a hollow voice, observing that he would probably throw his crutches away the moment her back was turned. He agreed cheerfully, "In that case, we'll put him into calipers." He picked up his gloves from the side table in the hall and nodded to Stephens, who had appeared soft-footed to let him out. "I'll be down on Wednesday, George—as near ten o'clock as I can manage."

He got into his car, waved in farewell, and disappeared, leaving her standing at the door, a prey to gloomy thoughts.

He was as good as his word; it was barely ten o'clock when he arrived. Georgina had not only readied Cor, but had thoughtfully cleared a space round the bed, and found a plain wooden table upon which to put all the clutter which they would presently discard. She had also prevailed upon Dimphena to take Beatrix down to the village for a good brisk walk. It had turned much colder in the last few days; there had been a little snow and a great deal of frost, but the sky was blue at the moment, and Beatrix had gone off happily enough with a list of odds and ends to buy for Georgina. Cor had been more difficult to deal with, though. He was white with excitement; he had eaten no breakfast and had objected more forcibly than usual to his bed-bath. He had begun, rather sullenly, to put forward a great many objections to crutches, calipers, or any support at all, and as the time approached for Mr. Sawbridge's arrival, he was declaring that the first thing he would do when he was on his feet would be to mount his bicycle. It was a great relief when Mr. Sawbridge, bearing several walking calipers under one arm, walked in. He greeted them cheerfully and said, "George, go down to the car and bring up the shoes, will you? We'll get this man on to his feet before I go."

"No crutches?" asked Cor, instantaneously good-natured again.

"No crutches," said Mr. Sawbridge, "provided you do exactly as you're told. Otherwise, crutches."

Georgina smiled as she sped downstairs. Old Sawbones was no fool; anyway he had little boys of his own. His car, a stately and somewhat elderly Daimler, stood before the door. Just behind it was the Silver Shadow, with the Professor bending his length over the boot. He looked up as she opened the door and observed, as though he were continuing a conversation which had been interrupted, "I've got several pairs of shoes here, for I daresay Cor's feet have grown. Stay there, I'll bring them—it's too cold for you to come outside."

She stood inside the door, watching him. He was half turned away from her, so that she could study him at leisure. It wasn't likely that she would have the opportunity to do so again and she didn't want to forget a single line of his face. When he straightened up she looked away quickly and stood aside to let him pass through the door, and then took the shoes from him while he took off his coat. She ventured to say to his back:

"I didn't expect you, Professor."

He turned to look at her. "I gave you no reason to do so," he remarked placidly. "Why did you stare so?"

Her composed voice successfully disguised her surprise.

"Was I staring? I'm sorry. I was thinking and not really looking."

He took the shoes from her. "A pity," he observed, and when she gave him an enquiring look, added, "That wasn't the answer I wanted."

They went up the staircase side by side, not speaking, and found Mr. Sawbridge in his shirtsleeves and Cor looking apprehensive. The Professor took off his jacket too, smiled encouragingly at his small ward, nodded to his colleague and said, "Right, let's go."

The wooden blocks upon which the foot of the bed had been resting had to be moved first. Georgina whisked them away as the men lifted and then unhooked the tins of shot which had weighted Cor's legs for so long, while the two men eased the cords attached to them. They kept up a steady flow of talk as they worked, so that when she went to the head of the bed and took hold of Cor's hand, he was almost unaware of Mr. Sawbridge drawing out the Steinmann pins from below each small knee, and anyway, he could see nothing of the small undertaking, as the Professor had placed his bulk strategically to block the view. . . . It was only left to remove the Thomas's splints to complete the business. This done, they paused for a moment to admire the little boy's strangely bony legs, though at least, as Julius was quick to point out, they were legs again; it only remained to get some muscle on them, and that would take no time at all.

"Let's see him go through his exercises, Nurse." Mr. Sawbridge glanced over to Georgina and smiled, and stood, still smiling, while she guided Cor to follow her painstaking work. When they had finished, she took Cor's hand and waited for the verdict.

"Very nice, don't you agree, Julius? Let's have him in a chair."

She had put a chair ready by the fire; now Julius scooped the little boy up and sat him in it, and she helped him into his dressing gown and knelt to put the socks on his feet while the Professor rang for Stephens. He held a low-voiced colloquy with him, and presently

Stephens came back with a tray with bottles and glasses.

"I think this calls for a celebration," said the Professor, "I suggest we drink your health, Cor, before we put on those calipers." The three of them solemnly toasted the boy, whose ill-humour had quite evaporated with his fears, and who now sat drinking apple juice from a sherry glass, and very cock-a-hoop. The calipers were comparatively easy after that. Georgina tied the last of the laces fastening the leather support of the calipers, winked encouragingly at Cor and stood back, while he walked, his guardian on one side, Mr. Sawbridge on the other, over to the window.

"Very good," said Julius. "Now let's walk back to Nurse."

She watched him make his way clumsily towards her, clutching the hands of the men on either side of him. The delight and excitement on his face were such that tears pricked her eyelids, and when he reached her at length, she caught him close and said shakily, "Oh, Cor darling, how well you manage!" She gave him a beaming smile, then smiled at the Professor too, who didn't smile at all but looked severe. Possibly he was annoyed at her want of dignity. She remembered how Gregg had warned her about her impetuosity; she should learn to control her feelings. . . . She checked a sigh and was grateful to Mr. Sawbridge when he said, "Success, I think, Staff Nurse Rodman, to which you have contributed more than your share." He spoke warmly. "Thank you for your co-operation. When you tire of Casualty, let me know—I can always use someone like you."

She could have hugged him. Instead she said, "Thank you, sir," went over to the table and started to tidy away the lengths of cord and paraphernalia. The Professor was on his knees, making some minor adjustment to Cor's calipers, and Mr. Sawbridge joined him. She listened to them talking quietly together, with occasional interruptions from Cor, and presently went downstairs with the spare calipers and shoes. When she got back, Mr. Sawbridge was in his jacket and ready to go.

He shook his patient's small hand, said, "Don't bother to come down, Julius, I want five minutes with Nurse, we can talk as we go," and followed her out of the room. On the way he asked, "How much longer are you staying, George?"

She looked straight before her. "I don't know, sir, but I don't expect it will be for more than a day or so. Anyone can fix those calipers and help him with bathing—Dimphena doesn't go to Switzerland for a few weeks yet."

He grunted. "Oh, well, I suppose Julius will decide. I take it you have no objection to staying on for a bit if he considers it necessary."

She said woodenly, "Of course not, sir," and he grunted again.

"Think well before you take that job in Casualty." He didn't explain his remark, and she was unable to ask because Stephens was helping him on with his coat.

The day was, naturally, not like any other day. For one thing, the Professor stayed home, and Karel arrived for lunch, a meal to which Cor was carried in triumph by his guardian, surrounded by his brother and sisters. It was a noisy meal with a great deal of chattering and laughter, and Georgina was glad when it was over, because the effort to be lighthearted was one she found difficult to sustain. She looked around the table and wondered how long it would be before she would be able to forget the three months she had spent at Dalmers Place and the people who lived in it, and realised that it would be never. She was fond of each one of them; and Julius she loved.

Mindful of Mr. Sawbridge's instructions, Cor was carried back to his room after the meal, and in the face of his determined opposition, she took off his calipers and tucked him up in bed.

"Make haste slowly," she said firmly. "Tomorrow morning you shall get up again, and no amount of black looks will change that, so be a dear boy and stop sulking. Here's your book. I'm going down to the village, I'll bring you back one of those drawing books I was telling you about. I expect we'll all have tea with you presently."

She was almost ready to go out when Beatrix tapped on the door.

"I suppose you wouldn't like company?" she enquired wistfully.

"Nothing I'd like better," said Georgina, "but put on that new anorak, poppet, it's cold enough for snow. Besides, it's so pretty."

They were half-way down the staircase before she saw Julius standing in the hall below. Beatrix took the last few steps at a gallop and threw herself at him. "I'm going out with George," she stated, "and I'm sure if you asked, she'd take you too." She danced back to Georgina, who had come to a halt at the bottom of the staircase. "Wouldn't you, George dear?"

Georgina was saved from answering this delicate question, for the Professor spoke first. "What a delightful suggestion," he remarked. "Unfortunately, I've a small matter to settle before teatime."

He smiled at them both, and it crossed Georgina's mind that he looked very like Cor when that young man was plotting mischief.

It started to snow as they came home, and Georgina went along to Beatrix's room to make sure that she had changed her shoes and brushed her hair smooth again, so it was that everyone was already in Cor's room by the time she had changed back into uniform and set her cap once more upon her neat head. She sensed an air of excitement as soon as she entered, heightened considerably by the fact that everyone was looking at her, while pretending not to do so. She went to pour the tea, and arranged Cor's meal on his bedtable in a spate of talk which did nothing to dispel the idea that they had all been talking about her. There was a lull in the conversation and she glanced up to catch the Professor's gaze fastened upon her, and was quite bewildered when he asked smoothly:

"Have you a passport, Miss Rodman?"

She shook her head; if this was an opening remark in a conversation she was going to find it difficult to keep her end up. It seemed a peculiar topic, but at least a safe one. "No, I haven't. I've not been out of England."

The much-travelled members of the Eyffert family turned a battery of blue eyes on to her.

"Didn't you ever want to go?" queried Beatrix.

"Yes, of course," began Georgina with some asperity, then paused. It was hardly their faults that she had never had the opportunity to travel. She smiled suddenly. "One day I shall go to Vienna and that bit of coast between Marseille and Spain—oh, and Paris on the way home."

She was looking at Beatrix as she spoke, but when the Professor asked, "In the meantime, would you consider coming to Holland with us?" she turned her brown eyes upon him; they were opened very wide, so was her delightful mouth. She stared at him, bereft of speech.

"You see," he went on very gently, "I want to take Cor over to Bergenstijn for a holiday, but I can't unless you will come with us. The others will come for a few days, and there may be guests.... We shall want you. Will you come?"

She had her breath back. "Yes, thank you. I should like to come very much." A succession of thoughts skidded through her brain. Her passport—clothes, and would she have time to see Aunt Polly before she went and what about free time while she was there and how were they going?

It seemed he was a mind-reader, for he said soothingly, "Don't worry about clothes or your passport. If you will come down to the study presently we can discuss the details." He smiled and she looked away, because when he smiled at her like that she loved him very much.

She had time to collect her thoughts before tea was finished. Everyone talked at once, making plans of their own, asking endless questions. She listened to everything that was said, but spoke little herself, and when Julius at length rose to his feet and suggested that she should accompany him, she got up readily enough, eager to hear the answers to the questions seething in her head.

In the study, he said, "Sit down, please," and went to his desk, where he began a search for something or other, tossing papers and books and pharmaceutical samples in all directions. She sighed and got up.

"I suppose you've written notes on the back of an envelope again," she remarked admonishingly. "Let me look—you can't hope to find it in this chaos." She gave him a severe look and began to sort through the mess. After a minute or two, she handed him the missing notes and sat down again. He took it meekly, observing, "Ah, you see it isn't only Cor who needs you." He was half smiling. "And do sit back comfortably. I shan't gobble you up, you know."

She blushed in the firelight, and sat back obediently, studying the toes of her neat shoes, listening to his pleasant voice as he told what had to be done. "Your passport—there's no time to get one. You can obtain a temporary one, though—we'll see about that tomorrow. You'll want to go home...." He thought a moment. "I'll run you over tomorrow evening after dinner, if that suits you. Clothes—well, Phena will tell you better than I. I daresay there'll be some skating—do you skate?" She nodded. "And bring that green dress you wore at Christmas."

His eyes were on the envelope so she didn't have to answer him, which was a good thing, for her heart had taken a sudden leap into her throat, so that she had no voice.

"We shall be there a couple of weeks, I expect—I have a meeting to attend in Brussels, and I may have to come back to England for a day or so, but Karel will come over for several days, and Dimphena and Beatrix will be there. You shall have a couple of days to yourself if you want to go sightseeing. I don't think there is anything else."

She said, "No, thank you, Professor," and got to her feet; presumably the interview was over. He had risen too and came over to where she stood. "There's one thing more. I can never thank you adequately for your care and kindness to Cor." His blue eyes searched her face. "Maybe one day I shall be able to think of some way in which I can repay you. In the meantime, I can only say 'Thank you'."

She fought for serenity; he was so very close. "There's no need for more than thanks, Professor. I'm as happy about Cor's legs as you are. I—I'm fond of him, you know that. And I've been very happy here, you know that too." She cast a fleeting glance at his face and said hastily, "You haven't said when we're to go."

His face wore its usual placid expression once more. "Er—no. We should manage to get away on Saturday, I think. We'll take the car to Harwich, and we can drive home from the Hook."

"Do you take the car too?"

"Heavens, no. Someone will bring the Aston-Martin up from Bergenstijn to meet us."

She was taken aback. "You mean to say that you have a Rolls-Royce here and an Aston-Martin in Holland?" She sounded disapproving, and he chuckled.

"Oh, dear! Don't subject me to a diatribe because I own more than one car... after all, think of the patients who would suffer if I had to walk everywhere."

She burst out laughing. "You are absurd! You make it sound as though having things is of no consequence."

He lifted an eyebrow. "My dear girl, of course it's of no consequence. I could manage very well without."

She said seriously, "Yes, I know you could," and walked to the door. Suddenly she wanted to go because being with him in some way she couldn't quite understand. He was at the door a second ahead of her. His hand closed over hers on its big ebony knob. He asked, "Have you decided to take the Sister's post in Casualty if it's offered to you?"

She lifted her eyes to his. "Yes, I shall take it," she said quietly, and waited while he opened the door to let her through.

CHAPTER 9

THE Professor drove her over to the cottage the next day, after dinner. During the short journey he had said very little and that casually. A brief comment on the successful acquisition of her temporary passport in Saffron Waldon that morning; a somewhat longer comment upon Cor's legs and then a few random remarks about the weather, which was bitingly cold and icy underfoot. But it seemed from his remarks that these miserable conditions were just what were needed to make skating at Bergenstijn possible; another day or so, and it would be ideal. Georgina darted a quick look at his profile and decided with some surprise that he meant it. Apparently the flurried snow and glassy roads were equally to his taste; he drove the Rolls with the same nonchalance that he would have shown on a deserted motorway in broad daylight. Or, she amended, he appeared to do so. He was the most relaxed driver she had ever known.

It was a surprised Mrs Mogg who answered the door to them, and a still more astonished Aunt Polly who greeted them when they went into the sitting room. She looked at them sharply, but all she said was, "What a delightful surprise!" She kissed her niece and shook hands with the Professor. "Georgina, will you go and ask Mrs. Mogg to let us have some coffee and some of those nice little biscuits she made today?"

Georgina went willingly. For one thing, she wanted to do something to her face and hair. She spent a few minutes before the mirror, and then, more or less satisfied, went to fetch the coffee tray from the kitchen. When she got back to the sitting room, the Professor had divested himself of his overcoat, and was sitting close to Aunt Polly, discussing wines, a subject they both appeared to find engrossing. He got up and took the tray and set it at Aunt Polly's elbow, and it wasn't until they were sitting with their coffee cups that he remarked:

"You must be wondering why we have come, Miss Rodman. Cor is more or less on his feet again, you know, and I plan to take him over to Holland for a short holiday, and we have persuaded—er—Georgina to come with us. Indeed, we could not do without her, for Cor still needs a firm hand if he is not to do too much, as well as a certain amount of nursing care. We plan to go on Saturday—by boat, you know. The journey to Harwich will take only an hour or so. We shall sleep on board."

If Great-Aunt Polly was taken aback, she gave no sign of it. She said merely, "What a treat for you, Georgina. I suppose it will be cold in Holland at this time of year—you'd better take some sensible clothing, dear." Georgina caught the Professor's eye and looked away quickly. She had been wearing uniform all these weeks; what could be more sensible than that? It seemed a good time to ask.

"Would you like me to continue wearing my uniform, Professor Eyffert?" she said, and was puzzled when he said blandly, "No. There is no longer any need."

She was on the point of asking why, when she encountered his look. His eyes were twinkling with laughter, but all he said was, "Did Phena give you some idea of what to take?"

"Yes, thank you. Perhaps I'd better go and get a few things...?"

She looked at her aunt, who nodded happily. "Do, dear, and while you're gone Julius shall tell me more about this home of his in Holland."

She went upstairs. For how long had her aunt been calling the Professor Julius, for all the world as if they were close friends or knew each a good deal better than their brief encounters justified? It made the fact that he almost invariably called her Nurse or Miss Rodman much harder to bear. She went to the attic and fetched her case, opened it on her bed, and started the serious business of deciding which clothes to take. In the end she chose a thick tweed skirt and a couple of sweaters to go with it, a pair of slacks, an apricot-coloured jersey dress, and a long-skirted pale blue Shetland wool dress; it had short sleeves and a turned-over, pointed collar— it would do very well for the evenings; the long, full skirt might be a good idea if Bergenstijn was even half the size indicated by Cor's drawings. She stood looking at the little pile of clothes and after some thought, took down one more dress—organza, the colour of milk chocolate. It had wide sleeves tied at the wrists, and a broad belt to define her neat waist; its collar was a froth of ruffles. It was a delicious dress and she wasn't sure if she would have a chance to wear it, but she packed it just the same.

Later on, when they were ready to leave, the Professor went upstairs with her to fetch her case. He stood in the middle of her room, studying it with deliberate interest. It was a pretty room, but as far as she could see, it hardly merited so much attention. When he at length picked up the case and went to the door, he observed coolly:

"Your room is charming—like its occupant."

She went downstairs behind him, her cheeks warm, her heart thumping in a maddening way, and angry with herself because of it, for of course, he meant nothing, nothing at all. It was a pity she couldn't convince herself of this once and for all. Probably he made himself agreeable to all the women he knew; her good sense told her so, even while she vainly tried to suppress the silly romantic notions rattling around in her head. They certainly got no encouragement on the way back, for he talked exclusively of the amazing recovery of a patient of his in the Intensive Care Unit at St. Athel's, so that the talk, though interesting, was quite impersonal. She wished him goodnight without warmth, and went up to bed, feeling waspish.

They left on Saturday, with Cor stretched out on the back seat of the Rolls with Georgina beside him, and the two girls in front with their guardian. Karel and Franz, who were to join them the following weekend, saw them off, with Mrs. Stephens and Milly beside them; of Stephens there was no sign, but the Leggs, squeezed together into their miniature doorway, waved as they passed by. The weather was colder than ever, the late afternoon sky was a uniform dull grey, and the ground like iron. Stephens' absence was explained when they arrived at the Customs at Harwich, for he appeared, rather like a genie from a bottle, as the Professor drew up. He had a wheelchair with him, and three porters. The Professor put his small cousin into the chair, said briefly, "Go inside, all of you. Stephens, come back when you're ready, please."

Georgina wasn't sure what she had expected—a queue perhaps, certainly some waiting about for tickets and luggage. She walked beside Cor's chair, keeping pace with Stephens' sedate tread. "Are you coming too, Stephens?" she asked.

He shook his head. "No, Miss Rodman. I'll be taking the car home presently, and be here to meet you when you return." He disposed the party in the waiting room, wished them a happy holiday and took his departure. They did not have long to wait; within a few minutes the Professor joined them, and in no time at all, it seemed to her, she was following him up the gangway with Beatrix clinging to one hand, and the rest of the party strung out behind them.

Once on deck, they were met by a steward, a stewardess and the purser, and thus escorted, reached their cabins. Georgina was a greenhorn when it came to travelling, but even she was able to see that the Professor, when travelling, did so with the effortless ease of the wealthy. It was a surprise to find that she was to have a cabin to herself. It communicated with the one shared by Dimphena and Beatrix. When she had looked around her she came to the conclusion that they weren't cabins at all, but staterooms. She was sure that cabins had bunks, and there was a dear little bed in her room, and twin beds in the girls'.

"Where's Cor?" she asked, and Dimphena pointed across the gangway. "Over there with Julius." She spoke rather absently, arranging her hair with all the anxiety of a sixteen-year-old. Georgina frowned. There had, of course, been a mistake. She stepped briskly to the half-open door opposite her own, and tapped. Cor was on one of the beds, bubbling over with some small boy's merriment; his guardian was sitting on the other bed, reading from a menu card. They both looked up as she went in and the Professor unfolded himself carefully to tower above her.

He said blandly, "Ah, Miss Rodman. Can I help in any way?"

She eyed him uncertainly. "Well—" she began, "I think there has been some mistake. Shouldn't I have Cor in my room?"

"No, I think not," he replied placidly. "You'll have more than enough of him in the next week or so."

This remark called forth fresh giggles from Cor. He smiled too, then continued, "The steward tells me that they are expecting a rough crossing—you'll be better on your own, especially as Cor is a good sailor. We two shall sleep like tops." He exchanged a grin with the little boy. "And if you don't feel—er—quite the thing, the stewardess can look after you without disturbing anyone."

She said, "Yes, of course. I hadn't thought of that." Annoyance that he could contemplate a sound night's sleep while she presumably might spend a wretched night battled with her awareness of the common sense of his suggestion. Nevertheless, she had her work to do. "I'll get Cor ready for bed, shall I, and see about his supper."

Her bosom heaved with indignation when he said on a laugh, "If it will make you feel better, my dear Miss Rodman. I'll go along and see about food . . . hot milk for Cor, I expect, and a sandwich?"

He wandered away, looking vague, leaving her with the shrewd suspicion that whatever she suggested, the whole journey would be carried out according to his own plans.

She got Cor undressed and in bed and then coaxed him to eat the light supper the steward had brought, and while he was busy with it, went in search of Beatrix, whom she found, wedged firmly between her guardian and her sister, watching the cargo being stowed under the great arc lights. When she saw Georgina she said, "Dear George—just five minutes more."

"No," said Georgina, at her most firm. "Now, my poppet," and bit her lip under the Professor's thoughtful stare, but all he said was, "Off you go, Beatrix, we shall all be up early in the morning, you know." He bent to kiss the little girl and smiled at Georgina so that her heart turned over.

Beatrix was excited too, but by the time she was sitting up in her bed she was already half asleep. She curled up presently and said coaxingly:

"Please stay a little while, George."

"All right, poppet; I'll just see if Cor's asleep."

He was, and as she came out of his stateroom the steward appeared at her elbow, soft-footed and pleasant.

"I'll keep an eye on the little boy, miss—you don't have to worry about him."

She went back to Beatrix who opened her eyes in a sleepy stare and closed them again on a childish murmur. She sat quietly, only turning her head when the door opened and the stewardess murmured that Professor Eyffert had asked her to keep an eye on the little girl, and withdrew again. There was no denying that the Professor looked after his own. Easy enough, she told herself, when you had money, and was instantly ashamed of the thought, knowing that he would look after his own whether he had money or not. Money had nothing to do with it.

Beatrix was fast asleep; there was no reason for her to remain any longer, but she wasn't sure what was expected of her. Julius hadn't actually said that she was to have supper with them—perhaps she was supposed to have something in her own stateroom and keep an eye on the children. But he had arranged for that. . . . She was trying to decide what to do when he came in. He glanced first at Beatrix, and then at Georgina who, because she felt she should say something, observed, "Isn't she beautiful?" and went pink and wished she hadn't, because he looked at her with the odd expression she had seen before. "'What would you like me to do, Professor?" she asked firmly.

He laughed softly. "As to that, my delightful Miss Rodman, I can think of several things . . . but shall we settle for supper? I've a table and Phena is waiting."

She went with him to the dining room, the thought uppermost in her mind the satisfied one that she was wearing her almost new tweed suit—it was a mixture of olive and cream and ginger, and it had its own creamy wool shirt. She was aware that she looked very nice in it.

"Hungry?" he asked, as they sat down.

"Yes," she said doubtfully, "but if it's going to be rough. . . ."

"It's much worse on an empty tummy," observed Dimphena, who, probably with this possibility in mind, was choosing a meal which would have satisfied a starving wolf. Georgina looked apprehensive and Julius laughed.

"That's only an excuse so that you can eat everything in sight! You'll get fat, Phena. No one will want to marry you."

She wrinkled her beautiful nose at him. "Oh, yes, they will, and even if they don't, I shall be quite happy living with you, Julius."

He looked up from the menu he was studying. "Oh, no, sweetheart. I intend to have a wife and a houseful of children."

"Julius, how lovely! I'll be an aunt. When shall you marry?"

He didn't look up this time. "That depends. . . . Now what about you, Georgina? Clear soup, I think, and then a grilled sole with creamed potatoes, and perhaps a crême brulée?"

She agreed politely, her erstwhile appetite impaired by the thought of him with a houseful of children. His wife would be a beautiful, slim creature. Her own delightful plumpness suddenly assumed vast proportions. She ate her simple meal with the virtuous thought that there wasn't a fattening morsel in it, and tried not to notice Dimphena's roast chicken or Julius's magnificent steak. But at least he allowed her a glass of Sauternes and some cognac with her coffee, so that by the time they had finished their meal, she was feeling more cheerful. The boat was on the point of sailing and Dimphena asked excitedly:

"May we go up on deck, just for a minute, Julius? I do love this bit when we leave the land behind."

Georgina caught her look. "Oh, yes that would be delightful." She looked at the Professor. "Shall we need our coats?"

"I'll fetch them and take a look at the children at the same time."

He was back almost at once, and they made their way on deck. Even out of the wind, it was cold, and once the boat was clear of the quay, increasingly rough. Georgina eyed the white-capped waves gleaming momentarily in the ship's lights as she began her battle across the North Sea, and was grateful to the Professor for choosing her meal so carefully. He stood between them, his arms around their shoulders, obviously enjoying the wild darkness. After a little while, Dimphena said, "I think I'll go to bed. George dear, do wake me if you want anything. Julius, are we to have breakfast before we land?"

"Yes—order tea for six o'clock, we'll breakfast at seven, and be away by eight—home for coffee."

It sounded funny to hear him say home, when his home was in England. Perhaps, thought Georgina, he was happier at Bergenstijn than Dalmers Place. She remembered Madame LeFabre; of course, if she lived in Holland, naturally he would prefer it. Perhaps he would live there permanently when he was married.

"A penny for them," he said.

Instead of answering, she said, "I think I should go to bed too."

He said "No," and nothing more, so that to break a silence she said, "Well, I wondered which house you preferred."

"I'm happy in them both," he answered instantly. "My life is so evenly divided between Holland and England that I'm equally at home in either. I believe you will like Bergenstijn very much, it's not in the least like Dalmers Place, but it has its own beauty and charm, and my family have lived there for so long that it is in my blood."

She asked diffidently, "Will you always live like this—with two homes?" then added quickly, "I'm sorry, I didn't mean to be nosey."

Before he answered he put his other arm around her. "You're getting cold; we must go inside." But he didn't move and she stayed quiet, feeling the warmth of his arms and listening to the steady beat of his heart under her cheek. He said at length, "I should like to. I cannot imagine leaving either Dalmers Place or Bergenstijn; I'm happy in them both, as I want my children to be happy, with their roots in both countries."

Georgina shivered, but not with cold, and he pulled her close and kissed her gently. "My poor girl, you must be frozen." He kissed her again, with the same gentleness—as though, she thought miserably, I were Beatrix—and took her arm and helped her over the heaving deck until they came to her door. He said, "Don't hesitate to call the stewardess if you need her. Goodnight," and was gone.

She went inside and shut the door. The ship was dancing madly, but she didn't notice it; she was choking down the knowledge that however highly Julius regarded her as a nurse, she need be in no doubt that as a woman she aroused in him no more than a kindly, amused tolerance, tinged with a kind of detached interest. She forced the fact down with the desperate resolution of someone swallowing a more than usually bitter pill, undressing as she did so. When she was ready she went to the mirror and peered at her reflection. It did nothing to reassure her, and in any case, she couldn't see it very clearly, because she was crying.

She spoke to its blurred image with severity. "You're not his type, my dear—admit it once and for all. And what's more, he really hasn't ever given you cause to suppose that you were." She blew her nose with vigour and lay down on the bed, but not to sleep. She would be seeing a great deal of Julius during the next two weeks; that meant that she would have to be the nurse engaged for Cor, and nothing else. That being settled she advised herself to think about something else, and opened her handbag; she would examine her Dutch money, or something. She had forgotten the letter; she had received it that morning, stuffed it into her bag and forgotten it. It was from St. Athel's. She opened it slowly, to find that it was from Matron, offering her the post of Casualty Sister, as from March the first next. She read it through several times, busy with her thoughts, so busy in fact that she quite forgot about seasickness and never noticed the gyrations of everything around her; indeed, after a while, she dozed off. When she awoke a couple of hours later, she made her way across the heaving floor to find her writing case. It was after four o'clock when her letter was finished. She washed and dressed and did her hair even more severely than usual, and sat quietly until the stewardess brought her tea. She was a pleasant woman, disposed to chat after a busy night.

"It's been a bad crossing," she observed. "I must say, miss, I was surprised you didn't ring for me—Professor Eyffert warned me particularly to come to you at once. Did you sleep?"

"Oh, yes," lied Georgina pleasantly. "This is such a delightful little room and I was tired. . . . I wonder would you post this letter for me when you get back to Harwich. I quite forgot it."

She gave it to the woman quickly, before she could change her mind, and asked if Dimphena had been called.

"No, miss, not yet. The steward has roused Professor Eyffert and the little boy, though, and he sent a message to say that if you wished to help the little boy, would you go over at half past six. I was only to give you it if you were feeling quite yourself." She smiled, "I must say you look very pale, miss."

"I'm excited, that's all," Georgina replied. "I'll go over at half past six—could someone let the Professor know, please?"

After the woman had gone, she poured herself a cup

of tea. Her letter would reach Matron the following day, or at any rate, the morning after. Her future was settled; she would have that to remember if the Professor should say or do anything to weaken her intentions. She finished her tea, and tapped on the girls' door, and presently was helping Beatrix to dress.

When she knocked on the Professor's door and went in, she found him in his shirtsleeves, brushing his hair, too. He turned to look at her and said shortly, "You haven't slept—were you sick? I told the stewardess to keep an eye on you but not to disturb you."

"I slept very well," she said cheerfully, "and I wasn't seasick, and no one disturbed me." But he went on looking at her in a rather unnerving fashion, so that she found herself rattling on, "What a pity it's so dark—I should have liked to see Holland from the sea." And then, because he still had said nothing, "Shall I come back presently?"

He spoke then. "No, I'll go. Send someone for me when Cor's ready."

It was easier when he'd gone; she was able to laugh and joke with Cor and even try out some of her peculiar Dutch at his insistent demand. Breakfast was all right too, because she sat between the two children, and their chatter precluded her from joining in any conversation with the others.

They were the last to leave the boat, so that there were no delays at all. They went through the customs; and then the restaurant; out on to the station platform and so to the road, to where the Professor, who had gone on ahead with the porters and luggage, was waiting by a dark blue Aston-Martin D.B.S. saloon. He stowed his passengers away with the same businesslike rapidity as the porters stowed the luggage, and Georgina found herself in the back seat with Dimphena and Cor wedged carefully between them. Beatrix he lifted into the seat beside him. He strapped her in securely, dropped a kiss on her small pink cheek, looked at his watch, and said over his shoulder:

"I'm going the quickest way. It's rather dull, but

160

we'll see that you go sightseeing later." He let in the clutch.

Perhaps it was dull for someone who had been there before. She stared out of the window and found a great deal that was distinctly foreign and strange. The houses were different; disappointingly square with old-fashioned sash windows, but the town was small; they left it by a wide road lined with villas, each standing in its own garden, windows glistening even on the grey windy morning. They had the neatness of well-cared-for doll's houses. It was strange, too, travelling on the wrong side of the road, although this didn't seem to trouble the Professor at all. They joined a main road presently, and then, a few miles further, the motorway to Rotterdam. Here the car came into its own, for there was no speed limit on the open highway; only as they reached Rotterdam did Julius slow down, giving her a chance to glimpse the great blocks of flats and streets of old houses with steeple roofs and red brick walls. It was still early, but there were plenty of people on the streets, and even more on bicycles; they leaned negligently against the car's sides each time they halted at traffic lights, and then pedalled away with an inch to spare with a *sang-froid* which the Professor shared, for he took no more notice of them than if they had been flies.

Georgina remarked on the people at such an hour on a Sunday morning, and the Professor said laconically, "Church," and gave his attention to driving once more. They left the city behind, and she was able to study the tranquil country they were passing through, it was a pity, though, that the road skirted the villages, for they looked charming, even at a distance, but when she remarked on this, the Professor merely observed, "I told you it would be dull."

Dimphena agreed that it was dull, but added, "Let's take George to Oudewater and weigh her on the witch's scales, and we can go to Gouda too." "And Delft," said Cor; and not to be outdone. "Amsterdam," Beatrix reminded them.

"All in good time," said Julius. "Here's Utrecht

161

ahead." They turned off at the great roundabout outside the city, however, and cut across it and on to the Maartersdijk road. The country had changed; it was delightful with little copses and meadows, intersected by narrow waterways, and when they had gone through Maartensdijk, it became even prettier, with lanes leading off from either side and houses amongst the bare trees. They passed through a cluster of houses and then down a winding lane, running between trees. There were one or two houses at first, and then nothing but the woods on either side, although it was only a few hundred yards before the Professor turned the car through a high old-fashioned wrought iron gate and on to a short drive, running as straight as a ruler to the house facing the gate. Georgina loved it at first sight. It was solidly square, with large sash windows and a vast front door, before which they stopped.

The Professor said over his shoulder, "Welcome to Bergenstijn, Georgina," and got out. It seemed that he was as well served here as he was in England, for the door had opened and an elderly man advanced to meet him. He had a faintly ecclesiastical air, due to a certain portliness and a quantity of snow-white hair allied to a splendid moustache. He shook the Professor by the hand and received a rapturous hug from Beatrix, who had climbed out of the car and was skipping around in wild excitement. He had a warm greeting from Dimphena too; Georgina began to wonder who he was and her unspoken thought was answered by Julius, who had come to fetch Cor.

"This is our house steward, Hans. He has been with the family for more than forty years and deals with everything. He is devoted to us all and we are just as devoted to him. Come and meet him."

She met the faithful Hans' searching blue eye with a smile and an outstretched hand and as he took it, he said formally in slow, difficult English, "I am happy to know you, miss." It was a relief to her when his many-wrinkled face broke into a smile, because somehow it mattered that he should like her.

Inside, the house was as unlike Dalmers Place as it

was possible to be. The rooms were large and square, like the house; with lofty ceilings and important fireplaces. A large house for a large man, thought Georgina, no wonder he liked it so much, the house and the man were made for each other. She was sitting in what the others had called the 'little room', drinking coffee in their company. It overlooked the gardens, and its windows were hung with plum-coloured curtains and topped with elaborately draped pelmets tied with thick silk cords. She had never seen anything like them outside the glossy magazines or the cinema. The carpet was plum-coloured too, but the deeply comfortable chairs and sofas were covered in cream velvet. She frowned a little, thinking of cleaning problems—probably there were no dogs in the house.... There were. They came in together, a Great Dane and a very small black dog, and made straight for the Professor, who made much of them before they deserted him for Cor, who was sitting beside Georgina.

She pulled gently on the big dog's ears. "What is his name?" she asked. "And that small creature. . . ."

"Anderson," Cor told her, "and this one's called Flip. He's a Schippershond." She repeated it after him, and he was too polite to laugh at her clumsy rendering of the word. "They live on boats," he explained, and she, none the wiser, would have probed the matter more deeply had it not been for the Professor getting up and coming over to say, "Lenie will take you to your room, Georgina. She's our housekeeper. She doesn't speak English, but Dimphena will go with you. You would like to unpack, I expect, and when you are ready, we will decide what is best for Cor, shall we?"

She got to her feet at once, and went up the staircase at the back of the tiled hall with Dimphena chattering beside her, and Lenie, a large, silent woman, walking ahead. The room she was shown into was large too, although it appeared smaller by virtue of the heavy mahogany furniture with which it was furnished. It was of the Empire period, its well-polished gleam offset by the pale green hangings and bedspread. The carpet was a dull pink, a colour echoed in the lampshades. There was a small open fire burning in the steel grate, and a high-backed chair drawn up to it. It looked welcoming—as welcoming as the bowl of hyacinths on the night table by the bed. Lenie caught her eye, and smiled her way across the room to a door in the wall. It led to a bathroom, and thence to the room Cor was to occupy.

Left alone, she unpacked a little, did her hair and her face and went downstairs again, to find everyone sitting much as she had left them. But the Professor got up at once and led her across the hall to another, smaller room with panelled walls and a massive desk set against its window. There were bookshelves everywhere, and a round closed stove whose warmth lent its surroundings an air of cosy intimacy. His study, she deduced, taking the smaller of the two chairs by the stove which she eyed with interest. It was almost a museum piece, of much decorated iron and capped with a metal cap that gleamed like silver. Being of a practical turn of mind, she wondered about its fuel consumption. Probably vast, she thought, and for the hundredth time wondered about the Professor's life; so very different from her own, even though he worked just as hard, if not harder, than she did herself.

Julius had stretched himself out in the leather chair facing her. He looked relaxed and contented, and when he smiled her heart began its familiar pounding. For a second she allowed the gossamer illusion that they were sharing their own hearth—their lives as well—to wreathe its hopeless way across her mind. Unable to help herself, she smiled back.

He said mildly, "That's better—you looked so forbidding; for one moment I thought you had taken a dislike to Bergenstijn."

She stirred, her brown eyes wide. "Dislike it? Here? But how could I, it's beautiful. The house when you first see it, and my room with those pink hyacinths and this lovely old stove—and I saw a lake from my window. . . ." She paused. It's covered in ice, just like the painting at the top of the staircase—the very small one next to the old gentleman with the wig." She went on, happily incoherent, "There's a ginger kitten asleep on the window seat outside my room." She smiled at the thought of it, and looked beautiful. "It's home, just as Dalmers Place is home. Some houses are, you know."

He smiled gently and with a triumph she didn't notice. "You are the most extraordinary girl. You find pleasure in things that a great many people don't even see."

She said shyly, "I think you do too."

He was serious now. "Yes, it matters to me, Georgina, that you should like my home."

His eyes were twinkling again; he was charming and kind and he was staring at her in a way she found disturbing. . . . She forced herself to meet his gaze coolly and before she could be trapped into saying something impulsive she might regret later, she observed in a thin voice :

"Well, yes, I suppose so. It's so much easier to work in a place you like."

The small sound which escaped his lips might have been a laugh; she wasn't sure. He said merely, "So you noticed the painting upstairs—it's a Van Ruydael, painted before this present house was built, though we still have the original cellars and an underground kitchen which isn't used any more. I'm delighted that you like your room, though I can't take any credit for the kitten asleep on the window seat."

They both laughed, and she felt the dangerous delight she always felt when she was in his company beginning to steal over her. She remembered her resolutions made during the night. "You wanted to give me instructions about Cor, Professor."

She thought he would never answer. And then, very blandly, "Do you disapprove of me so very much, Miss Rodman?"

She felt her face grow hot. She stuttered indignantly, "Disapprove of you? Me? Of course I don't. What a ridiculous notion! And why do you say that?" she demanded.

He was laughing again. "You are so very anxious not to waste time with me—a fact I greatly deprecate."

She looked at him helplessly, for there was nothing to say. To agree with him would be easy and untrue; to disagree would mean that he would want to know why. . . .

"How unkind of me to tease. I'm sorry." He spoke lightly without looking at her, and settled himself deeper in his chair, crossed one long leg over the other and contemplated his shoes. "Now, this business of Cor."

Between them, they drew up a simple routine for the little boy. There was always the danger that he would do too much now that he was on his feet again. That had to be prevented while at the same time he mustn't feel that he was being pampered. There would, it seemed, be guests coming on Wednesday—he gave no names—and Karel and Franz would arrive on the following Sunday and stay for several days. Cor would need a firm hand and constant supervision. When they had finished, Georgina said jokingly:

"Now I know why you were so anxious for me to come." She got up. "I'll get the children ready for lunch."

He went to the door with her, saying casually, "You are free to think whatever you wish of my reasons for wanting you to come, Georgina. At the moment, I have no intention of telling you."

They all lunched together, and a round-faced dumpling of a girl with flaxen hair and bright round eyes served them. Dimphena introduced her as Pankie, which Georgina found rather peculiar until it was explained that it was a shortened form of Pancratiana, which, upon reflection, she found even more peculiar. She shook hands and said with great difficulty because she was shy of speaking any language other than her own, "*Goeden Dag*, Pankie," and was rewarded by a shout of triumph from her youthful teacher and more subdued applause from the others, who, throughout the meal, egged her on to air what she had learned, sometimes with the most amusing results.

Afterwards Cor, protesting hotly that he had no desire to rest, was carried up to his bed, but when he found that Beatrix and Georgina were to accompany him, he submitted with a good grace to having his calipers taken off and being tucked up, while Georgina did the same for Beatrix on the day bed under the window. This done, she poked up the fire, produced a copy of *The Tale of Benjamin Bunny* and began to read. The children were asleep within ten minutes, leaving her free to curl up in her chair and stare at the flames. Presently she would write a long letter to Aunt Polly and another one to the girls at St. Athel's; tomorrow she must buy postcards; perhaps there was a shop in the little village they had gone through. . . . Her eyes closed.

She awoke on a dream—a delightful one in which she was being kissed by Julius. The joy of it was still real in her mind when she opened her eyes and found him standing beside her chair. Just for a moment dream and reality were a pleasurable whole, then she discarded the dream, sat up, looked at the sleeping children and asked:

"Is anything the matter? I must have dropped off."

He had his hands in his pockets, his face very placid. He answered softly, "Nothing is the matter—it's tea-time."

She got up. "Oh, then I'll wake the children and bring them down. I can't think why I went to sleep."

"Surely a natural thing to do," he answered smoothly, "when you have had a sleepless night."

"Yes—I was very tired." She stopped, remembering clearly that she had told him that she had had an excellent night's sleep. She peeped at him through her lashes to see if he had noticed and saw that he had. His face wore an 'I told you so' expression which was maddening. She repeated, "I'll wake the children," and did so, leaving him to sit in the chair while she combed their hair and tidied them and fastened Cor's calipers. She avoided him for the rest of the day, and went upstairs early after dinner, pleading letters to write.

She awoke the next morning to a world of cold and ice and blue sky and a feeling of happiness engendered by the knowledge that she would be seeing Julius every day for the next two weeks. She drank the tea Pankie brought, bathed and dressed and then set about getting Cor on to his feet. She was fastening the last strap of his calipers, with Beatrix in voluble attendance, when the Professor came in. He wished her a genial good morning, suffered a strangling embrace from Beatrix, and carried Cor down to breakfast.

Barely an hour later they were all down by the lake, watching while Julius tested the ice. Satisfied, he put on his skates and skimmed over its entire surface. He was an excellent skater. Georgina watched him; in a tremendous sweater, his wool-gloved hands clasped behind him, weaving to and fro until finally he came back to them and pronounced the ice safe. Presently he set off again with Beatrix, leaving Dimphena to execute graceful patterns on her own, and Georgina to walk Cor gently up and down the hard-packed snow at the lake's edge. They paused frequently to watch the skaters, especially Dimphena, who floated round with the practised ease of a dancer, her pretty face framed in a fur bonnet, her scarlet slacks and anorak making a vivid splash of colour.

They all came to a halt when Hans came down from the house with a great thermos jug of hot chocolate. He waited while they drank it, and then took charge of Cor, and Georgina, with a pair of Dutch Runners strapped to her stout shoes, found herself on the ice, with the Professor beside her. She hadn't skated for a couple of winters at least, and she faltered a little as they started off, but he slid a great arm round her waist and drew her along willy-nilly, so that in a few seconds she was quite at her ease, and by the time they had circled the lake she was enjoying herself hugely. The cold air rushed against their faces, the ice beneath their skates was smooth, her cheeks glowed and her eyes sparkled. She became as warm as toast and when they finally stopped and Julius pulled her round to face him, she said happily, "That was marvellous!"

He glanced at her, and then away. "You skate well. Do you know that you look pretty too?"

Her pink cheeks became pinker. She said in a little

girl's voice, "Oh, do I?" Her sheepskin jacket and brown knitted bonnet and her last year's tweed slacks hardly seemed the height of fashion to her, especially when compared with Dimphena's outfit. "I'll take Cor indoors, I think. It's time for his exercises." He was still holding her hand; he didn't let it go, but took her over to the edge of the ice and took off her skates. As he went he said, "We'll do this again."

He was as good as his word. The following morning, Cor, it seemed, wanted to spend an hour or so with Hans and Dimphena declared that she must go calling on friends and took Beatrix with her. Georgina found herself free to accept the Professor's invitation to skate. They circled the lake slowly while they talked; the easy talk of two people with all the world in common. She found herself telling him about her childhood with Aunt Polly and of how much she owed her. She said deliberately:

"That's why I've accepted Casualty Sister's post."

He halted so suddenly that she would have fallen if he hadn't been holding her firmly.

"You've what?" His voice was silky, there was something in its tones which made her look up at him. Her brown eyes met his blue ones and held them squarely. "You didn't tell me," he said flatly.

"I gave the letter to the stewardess to post in Harwich when she got back." She kept her voice level. "It's—it's what I've always wanted."

His eyes weren't blue any more. They had turned to steel and were just as cold. She wondered what he would say and was totally unprepared for his next remark.

"Did I tell you that we have guests tomorrow? A pity we shan't be able to skate again—by the time they leave, I expect a thaw will have set in." His voice was level, and she hoped that hers was equally so.

"It was wonderful." She swallowed a misery which was no easier to bear because she had deliberately brought it upon herself, and went on brightly, "I hope it doesn't thaw before Karel and Franz arrive."

He answered carelessly; she could see that she hadn't

got his attention. "I daresay it will hold until then. By the way, I must ask you not to go on the lake, either alone or with the children, until you have checked with me that it's safe." He looked at his watch. "Shall we go round once more before we go in?"

The magic had gone. He talked pleasantly about the house and the grounds and the small farm abutting his land, which he owned too; but he was a thousand miles away from her, and she realised sadly that now guests would be in the house, she would see less of him. After a little while she said timidly, "I'd like to go in now, please," and his "Of course" was so willingly said that her eyes sparkled with tears which she had no intention of shedding. They walked back to the house, and parted in the friendliest possible fashion in the hall.

They met again at lunch, and again during the pleasant half hour in the salon before dinner, when the whole family foregathered to chat about their day. She had expected him to ignore her as far as good manners would allow, she certainly didn't expect him to go out of his way to talk to her. She couldn't have been more wrong. He kept her by his side, discussing where she should go, and what she should see, and even complimented her upon the blue dress. And when she went upstairs to see Cor and Beatrix safely to their beds, he insisted, with a charm which yielded nothing to her excuses, that she should go down again. It was certainly pleasant with just the three of them. The Professor and Dimphena discussed their guests and their plans for entertaining them, taking care that Georgina was included in their talk. There was to be a luncheon party, to which some local friends would come, and a family dinner party as well, "And," said Dimphena hopefully, "perhaps a little dancing afterwards, Julius?"

"Why not?" he agreed lazily, "though remember that most of the family are too elderly to do anything more modern than the foxtrot." They all laughed, and he went on, "I think we should tell Georgina who will be coming. It will be less confusing. There will be Uncle and Aunt Van der Berg—fiftyish—they live in Wassenaar; then Uncle and Aunt Kuppers-Eyffert, who come from a small place near Arnhem, and some cousins of mine—doctors, I'm afraid—and their wives, of course. There will be some children too—nice for Beatrix and Cor." He turned to Dimphena. "It's short notice, Phena, but I telephoned Therese LeFabre this afternoon. She will be coming some time after lunch. She can have the little bedroom at the end of the corridor."

Dimphena looked upset as well as surprised. "But, Julius, you said you were never...."

He gave her a blank look which brought her up short. "Did I really?" He smiled. "Poor Phena—but Therese knows us well enough to take pot luck."

Georgina found that the evening held no pleasure for her any more; which was stupid and illogical of her, her common sense assured her. She had known about Madame Lefabre, hadn't she? She had known that Julius would almost certainly see that lady while he was in Holland, so why should she feel as though the world had come to an end for her? She rearranged the folds of her long blue skirt meticulously with fingers that trembled despite her efforts.

"By the way," said Julius, and she looked up to find his eyes upon her; they gleamed with an expression she was unable to read, "Uncle Ivo—my Great-Uncle Ivo—will also be coming. He's eighty, and proud of it, and he is very prone to speak his mind. He is also very wise."

She went to bed soon after, because she didn't want to be left alone with the Professor. She said her good-nights and went upstairs, aware that he had known what had been in her mind about Madame Le Fabre. She got into bed, determined to think of nothing but her bright future at St. Athel's. But it was no good and she gave herself up to speculation about Therese LeFabre and presently she began to think about Julius.

CHAPTER 10

THE visitors arrived in ones and twos, the aunts and
uncles in chauffeur-driven cars, the cousins later in the
day, in small fast cars which pulled up before the house
with a good deal of horn blowing and squealing of
brakes. Neither of them were quite as large as Julius,
but they had his straw-coloured hair and blue eyes and
the same placid manner, which Georgina was beginning
to realise wasn't always as placid as it seemed. Their
wives were young, neither of them good-looking, but
possessed of a charm which could, on occasion, turn
them into beauties. They both had an excellent taste in
clothes, and the one was as dark as the other was fair.
Between them they brought four children, small, well-
mannered and gratifyingly curious about Cor's calipers.
They gravitated without urging to Georgina, and she
was pleased, for she was able to try out her rudimen-
tary Dutch on them. She didn't mind them laughing at
her in the least, and it amused them to correct her.

Before luncheon she went upstairs to repair the
ravages to her person consequent on the entertainment
of six small children, and it was as she was coming
downstairs again that she saw the old gentleman in the
hall. She knew who it was immediately, for Julius had
a likeness of him, in spite of the white hair and the
slight stoop. She looked around for Hans, but there was
no sign of him, and the old gentleman caught sight of
her and burst into resounding and incomprehensible
speech. She advanced to meet him, saying inadequately,
"How do you do? I'm afraid I cannot understand a
word you say."

He waited until she was close to him, then produced
a pair of old-fashioned gold rimmed spectacles the better to examine her. He took them off again before he
said, "So you're the girl Julius told me of." His English
was as good as her own and delivered in a deep rumb-

ling voice. "Nice-looking too," he went on, "plenty of flesh on your bones—can't bear skinny women myself, nor can Julius." Georgina blinked, but was saved from replying, for he hadn't finished. "You've got an outlandish name."

"Georgina," she said faintly. "Georgina Rodman. I'll tell Professor Eyffert that you're here."

Before she could move, he bellowed mildly, "Good God, girl, do you call him that all the time?" He looked down his nose a ther, making his resemblance to his great-nephew more marked than ever. "Afraid of me?" he asked.

"My goodness, no. Why should I be?" She smiled at him and watched the answering smile on his pleasant old face ,as he pronounced :

"You're a nice girl. Why doesn't Julius. . . ."

"Why don't I what, Uncle Ivo?" He came across the hall and shook his uncle's hand. "It's good to see you again. I see you're already met Miss Rodman."

"Is that what's she's called? I shall call her Georgina—that is provided she has no objection."

"None at all," she answered in a composed voice. She took care not to look at Julius, even when he said, "Shall we join the others?" and ushered them into the salon.

Therese Le Fabre arrived during tea. The children had spent a noisy happy afternoon playing in the snow, and Georgina had played with them while their parents tried out the ice. They were all warm and pleasantly tired when they joined the less mobile members of the party in the little room for tea. She sat the children together, supplied them with food and drink and went to ist by Uncle Ivo, who while making an excellent tea, asked a great many questions of her. She did her best to anwser them and was just wondering how to counter his forthright enquiry as to why she had not married, when Hans opened the door, and a woman came in. It had to be Therese, for she was everything Georgina had expected her to be, and even more than that. She was strikingly good-looking, as slim as a wand, and looked as though she had stepped straight from the pages of

Vogue. She paused with studied grace just inside the door, stretched out her arms with a tinkling of bracelets and cried in a ringing voice, "Julius!"

He had got up and was advancing to meet her with every appearance of pleasure. Georgina, suddenly cold inside, extracted a small scrap of comfort from the fact that he only took one of the outstretched hands and shook it. But that was really no comfort, for she didn't imagine that he was a man to kiss a girl in front of a roomful of relatives. She looked away and encountered the penetrating gaze of her companion.

He said softly, without taking his eyes from hers, "She's been after him for years—she's thirty if she's a day and no shape at all." He gave a whispered snort, which was none the less ferocious. "All those damned jingling bracelets!" He added fiercely, "I hope he knows his own mind."

Georgina hoped so too, but this was hardly the time nor the place to give the matter thought. She sought to lead Uncle Ivo's thoughts into pleasanter channels.

"I think she's lovely," she said evenly, intent on betraying nothing of her feelings. "Don't you like modern clothes?"

"Of course I like them—I'm not an old woman, even if I am eighty." He put his spectacles on and stared at her through them. "You're as transparent as glass, my dear," he said, suddenly gentle. "I hope you've got a pretty dress for dinner tonight."

She said lightly, "I've no intention of competing," and smiled widely. "I promised I'd play the piano for the children in the nursery. If they've finished their teas, I'll take them upstairs now, I think."

She went unhurriedly to fetch them and was almost at the door, ushering the last child through it, when the Professor reached her.

"Before you go, my dear Miss Rodman, come and meet Therese Le Fabre." His voice was silky. "A very old friend."

She shook hands, and was overwhelmed by charm, turned on deliberately and impossible to ignore. It was cloying and spiced with small pinprick remarks which somehow contrived to make Georgina feel a prig and someone to be pitied. She smiled her way through the conversation, glad that Julius had left them alone, although probably being a man, and in love, he would have noticed nothing. She followed the children upstairs, and said, "Oh, dear, love is so very blind!" which mystified the children considerably.

Blind or not, and very much on the losing side, she had every intention of going down with all flags flying. She put on the brown organza and, watched by Beatrix and Cor, spent a good deal of time arranging her hair in a shining pile on the top of her head. Therese would doubtless be loaded with jewels, and they would be real, she had no doubt; she fastened some early Victorian earrings—little golden tassels—into her pretty ears, and went to find someone to take Cor down.

The Professor was the only occupant of the salon when they entered. He was standing in front of the fire, with a glass in his hand, looking distinguished and remote. He looked up and watched as Georgina settled Cor in a small armchair, thanked Hans for his good offices, and arranged cushions where they would be most comfortable. When she had finished, she said, "There. Now I'm going to see if Beatrix is ready...."

"No," said the Professor, "stay here." He spoke so gently that she wasn't sure if she had heard him at all. "Phena is quite capable of helping Beatrix with buttons and things," he went on. His deliberate glance swept her from head to foot and she willed herself to remain calm under it. She knew she looked nice—the brown organza was becoming in its own modest fashion.

He said abruptly, "How delightfully feminine you look," and went over to the sofa table behind the great sofa to fetch her a drink. She thanked him with a coolness wholly at variance with her heightened colour, and sipped, thankful to have something to do. She was cudgelling her brains for a topic of conversation when the door opened and Therese Le Fabre came in. She was wearing a silver trouser suit and a great many chains and rings; she made Georgina feel like a mouse. She stopped when she saw Georgina and Cor and said in her prettily accented English:

"Oh, you're here already," and then cast a speaking glance at the Professor. "Julius?"

He was looking at her with no expression on his face at all; now he smiled faintly and walked over to the drinks tray. "Your usual, Therese?" he asked pleasantly; if he was annoyed at not being alone with her, he was concealing his feelings very well.

Georgina got up and went over to Cor's chair, and sat down beside him, half-turned away from the others and by concentrating hard upon what he was saying, was able to ignore the murmur of their voices, and presently, when everyone else arrived, she was caught up in a small circle consisting of the doctors and Great-Uncle Ivo, who made no bones about admiring her appearance in a loud and penetrating voice.

The dinner was long and leisurely and delicious; if it hadn't been for Therese sitting beside Julius at the great oval table, Georgina would have loved every minute of it. As it was, she was glad when they at last left the table to stroll in little groups back to the salon, the children dragging a little by now, the men left behind to drink their port. She looked at Cor worriedly. He was tired—too tired. The treat of staying up late was wearing thin. She drank her coffee, and said firmly, "Bed, Cor dear."

He looked stubborn. "Not until all the others go too."

"They're coming," she said, and went to drop a word in motherly ears so that within a few moments she had the small creatures collected, with good nights said. They were at the door when Therese Le Fabre said:

"But it is wonderful, Miss Rodman; all these children who listen to you—you must be a very good nursemaid."

Georgina had been about to lift Cor to carry him upstairs—he wasn't heavy, and she wasn't going to disturb the men. She put him down again, her eyes sparkling with temper. She wasn't sure what she was going to say, in any case she had no chance to say it, for the Professor's voice, level and cold, spoke first.

"Miss Rodman is not a nursemaid, my dear Therese. She is highly skilled nurse without whom we should have been lost. She has no need to do anything at all for the children; it is her nature to help others."

Georgina felt herself enveloped in the warm and unwelcome glow from an all-embracing blush, which was not improved by Therese's gentle voice.

"Oh, my dear, I had no intention of being rude, believe me. I am so envious of you—that you can do so much for others and that the children are so fond of you. Alas, I have no children whom I can love."

This incredible speech was accompanied by two tears running, without harming her make-up, down her cheeks. She dabbed them away with a wisp of a handkerchief and smiled wistfully. Georgina watched her with embarrassment and pity. It must be awful, she thought, to have been married and not to have had any children. She said kindly, "Of course you weren't rude, and please don't get upset—you're much too beautiful," and stiffened when Julius said in a matter-of-fact voice, "Phena will give you a hand, Miss Rodman." She started to protest, but thought better of it when she saw his face; he was very angry and hiding it most successfully. She didn't think that anyone else there had noticed it, but over the past weeks she had come to recognise the blank look on his face when he was annoyed.

It took no time at all to get the children to bed. She left Cor till last because there were several things she had to do for him. It was while she was tucking him up that he said, "She meant it, you know, dear George."

"Meant what—and who?"

He muttered grumpily, "Madame LeFabre, of course. She was being beastly."

She said comfortably, "You're too tired to know what you're saying. Go to sleep, my dear." She kissed him and went to find Dimphena, to tell her that she wouldn't go back to the salon with her. "I've a headache," she invented, "and there'll be plenty to do tomorrow, I expect...no one will notice."

Dimphena went, looking doubtful, and presently she went back to Cor's room—there was a strap on one of his calipers which needed adjusting. She sat down on the floor before the fire, not caring about the brown organza getting creased—it hadn't worked a miracle anyway. She might just as well be in uniform. It had served her right for trying to attract his interest when he was practically engaged to someone else. She gave the cord which fastened the caliper's leather support a vicious tug and it broke. She sat and looked at it, and would have gone on looking at it for some time if the door had not opened behind her. Julius came across the thick-piled carpet and said quietly, "What are you doing?"

She had to look up a long way to see his face, and even then it was indistinct in the darkened room.

"This needed adjusting," she said in a voice which held only the ghost of a wobble. She held up the cord. "I broke it." She got up. "I've some spare ones in my room."

She fetched one and found him still there when she returned. He took it from her and threaded it quickly and laid it by its fellow.

"Phena tells me you aren't coming down again." His voice was gentle. "Will you change your mind?—we're going to dance."

She was about to say no, when it flashed through her mind that perhaps Therese had sent him, anxious to make sure that she hadn't really been offended. She smoothed her brown skirts. "Very well," she said, "I'll come."

It wasn't so bad—she danced a great deal, and twice revolved gently round the room with Great-Uncle Ivo. A number of people she hadn't met seemed to have drifted in—she supposed that they were local friends. She danced with everyone who asked her until just after midnight, when she slipped quietly away, confident that no one had seen her go. She was half way up the staircase when the Professor said from the hall below, "I haven't danced with you, Georgina."

She paused with her hand on the rail, and looked down at him. "No," she said. "Goodnight." She turned away and was barely a step higher before he was beside her.

"You don't ask why," he said mildly.

She didn't look at him. "I don't have to."

He caught her hand, so that she was forced to stand still. "If you ask me—now—I promise I'll give you the answer."

But she only shook her head. "Goodnight," she said again, and went on up the stairs alone.

She scarcely saw him the next day, and when she did, they hardly spoke because Therese Le Fabre was always with him.

The weather changed imperceptibly during the night; the cold north wind died away, although the sky remained a uniform grey and the snow looked as thick as ever. Georgina gave Cor his exercises, strapped on his calipers and took him for a sober walk, with the other children tearing round them like playful puppies. When they got back the first of the lunch guests had arrived. She got the children organised with her usual calm good sense, and went upstairs to change, returning presently wearing the apricot jersey. There was no sign of the children; she stood in the doorway of the salon, watching its laughing and chattering occupants, and took a step backwards into the hall, intent on discovering where they had got to. Cor still needed to be careful, but he wouldn't allow the fact to stop him if he was bent on mischief with the other five.

"Don't worry about the children, I've wished them on Hans for half an hour," said the Professor from the hall. "Come and meet some friends of mine."

He led her across the room to where Dimphena was talking to a very tall and generously built girl, and an even taller man. The Professor hailed them. "Maggy—Paul, this is Georgina, this is Maggy Doelsma, and her husband, Paul—a doctor, of course. Maggy was Ward Sister at St. Ethelburga's."

He stayed for a few minutes and then went away, taking Paul and Dimphena with him, leaving the two young women to talk. Maggy turned a pair of magnificent brown eyes on to Georgina and asked:

"Do you like it here—Holland, I mean?"

"I don't really know," Georgina answered. "I haven't been anywhere yet. I love Bergenstijn though—it's so different from the Professor's home in Essex, but just as nice."

Her companion eyed her with interest, said "Um," in a noncommittal way and then, "Do you like Julius? Is he nice to work for?"

"Very." This at least was a question she could answer easily. "He's most considerate, and the children are darlings."

Maggy nodded. "Aye; it's time he married and had some of his own, though." She looked around her. "I see Therese LeFabre is here—as elegant as ever and looking every day of her thirty years. Do you like her?"

Georgina answered guardedly. "She's very charming—she wears lovely clothes too. It must be awful to be left a widow...."

Maggy made a funny little sound between a snort and a laugh. "Not for her it isn't. She married a Belgian industrialist who left her a great deal of money, and I doubt she grieved overmuch. I don't like her."

"No," said Georgina simply, "nor do I."

They smiled at each other and after a pause Maggy asked, "When are you going back to St. Athel's? Julius said something about you getting Cas."

"Yes, from March the first. I think we go back to England at the end of next week. I suppose I'll go back to St. Athel's then."

"You must have a day with us before you go. I'll ask Julius to bring you over."

"No," said Georgina quickly. "I mean, I'd love to come, but the Professor has guests."

"All gone by Monday. We're not far away—Leiden."

"I—I don't know. Perhaps I could come by train?"

"Nonsense, I'll fetch you. Shall I give you a ring in a day or two?"

They went to lunch then, and she didn't see her new friends again except to bid them a brief goodbye. As they walked to their car, she saw Paul catch at his wife's hand, and the look he gave her, and suffered a pang of pure envy.

Karel and Franz arrived on Saturday in the fore-noon, cheerful, noisy and hungry, Georgina was in the hall when they arrived and Karel dropped his bag and came across the hall and caught her up and swung her in the air. "Georgina, more beautiful than ever! I shall expect the first dance with you this evening."

He put her down and gave her a smacking kiss and she giggled.

"Karel, do grow up! And I'm sitting out the first dance with Cor. I promised. The children are to stay up for an hour, you know."

"In that case, the second," he cried, and caught hold of her and waltzed her round the hall. It was at that moment that she saw Julius watching them from the study door. Karel saw him too, for he stopped with a flourish in front of him and said gaily, "Hullo, Julius. Here we are, you see. Bergenstijn seems to agree with Georgina, if her dancing is anything to go by."

She smoothed herself down so that she wouldn't have to look at the Professor, who said smoothly, "Hullo there. You must ask Georgina what she thinks of Bergenstijn presently, but come in now and tell me all the news of Dalmers Place."

He smiled at her briefly and closed the door gently.

She put the green dress on again that evening. The dance was to be a cosy affair, just family, with friends dropping in after dinner. But Dimphena was adamant that everyone should dress up for it. They dined early, so that the children should have their share of the evening's fun, and Georgina was delighted to find her-self between Karel and Great-Uncle Ivo. They talked a great deal of nonsense and laughed a great deal, and she tried not to look too often at Therese, who was wearing a pale chiffon caftan and what Georgina didn't doubt were real pearls. She looked gorgeous. Georgina stole a look at Julius, to encounter his bright stare upon herself, and turned away hastily with a flushed face, aware that he was secretly amused about something— probably her.

The salon was comfortably crowded when she collected the children and took them upstairs to bed. With Pankie's help she had them tucked up and was back in the salon within the hour, to dance with a gratifying number of partners. It was almost eleven when she slipped away and started up the big staircase again. She had almost reached the top, when the Professor called, "Georgina, where are you going?" And this time he followed her up and walked beside her along the corridor.

"It's all right," she said matter-of-factly, "I'm going down again. I promised Cor I'd come and peep at him, to make sure that he's asleep—Beatrix too."

She swept ahead of him and bent over each child in turn, then went along the little passage at the end and started up the small staircase at its end leading to the next floor. He kept pace with her, merely saying:

"You're going somewhere else."

She looked back at him and said serenely, "Why, yes. I told the children's mothers that I would look in on them while I was up here. There's no point in us all coming up."

She went in turn to the two bedrooms, where she found one small girl awake and went through the ritual of a drink of water, and the turning of the pillow and the re-tucking up. Finally she dropped a kiss on the round cheek and rustled softly past him, leaving him to shut the door. They were almost at the head of the stairs again when he said, "Georgina," and she stopped and looked round, to be instantly clasped and kissed and kissed again, until, almost unknowingly, she returned his kisses. But presently she put a firm hand against the fine stuff of his dinner jacket, remembering Therese, and said in a steady, cold voice:

"You've been wanting to do that, haven't you? Perhaps you'll feel better now."

Through her own pain she heard the shock in his voice, as he repeated:

"Better? What the devil do you mean by that?"

She said tiredly, "Just what I say. When you can't have something it gets out of all proportion, doesn't it? You want it all the more even though you don't really want it . . ." She stopped, for she was getting muddled; all the same, she felt that she had made herself clear. Apparently she had, for he let her go.

"You think that?" He spoke in a calm almost casual voice that told her nothing.

She repeated, "Yes, I mean that. Goodnight."

She made herself go calmly down under his eye, longing, most illogically, for him to say something—anything. He said nothing at all, and although she stayed stubbornly until the last guest had gone, he didn't speak to her again.

Only Karel and Franz were at breakfast when she went down with the children; and they were off somewhere for the day. She listened to their talk and replied suitably, and when they had gone realised that she hadn't heard a word they had been saying. Everyone was leaving that morning—it was Great-Uncle Ivo, bidding her a courtly goodbye, who let drop the news that Julius had gone out very early that morning to some urgent call from a hospital in Amsterdam. She stood with Dimphena and the two children, waving goodbye, and asked as she turned away, "Is Madame LeFabre staying on?"

Dimphena replied rather shortly, "Yes. She's afraid it will be too dull for Julius over the weekend. She says she will cheer us all up. I heard her arranging to meet Julius for lunch today, so I expect we shall have to do our own cheering up."

She looked resigned and Georgina said bracingly, "Why don't you look up that friend who couldn't come yesterday—surely Karel would give you a lift?"

Dimphena brightened, and thus petitioned, her brother willingly agreed, and half an hour later, having seen them on their way, Georgina stood in the hall in slacks and jacket and a bright scarf on her head, while the two children debated their morning's amusement. It was overcast outside, with no wind at all, and Beatrix, always persistent, reiterated her demand to skate.

"What about Cor?" asked Georgina. "It won't be much fun for him."

"Yes, it will, if we stop and talk to him every time we go round," persisted her small companion. "Half an hour," she wheedled, "please, dear George."

"Your guardian said we weren't to skate unless he gave permission, and you know he went far too early this morning for me to see him."

"Ah, but I have seen him," said Therese from the stairs. She hurried towards them, saying diffidently, "I overheard you as I came down—you do not mind, I hope? But you see Julius gave me a message for you, that you might skate if you wish. He thought that perhaps you feel lonely now that everyone is gone. It was, you understand, far too early for him to tell you himself." She glanced at Georgina and gave a half smile. "It is good for skating; no wind. If I have the time before I meet Julius, I may join you."

She drifted away, leaving an aura of something delicious behind her. When she had quite gone, Cor said, "Let's go, George. I don't mind standing, and I can walk along that little path Hans cleared for me; only let's go indoors again if she comes too."

They started for the door. Georgina smiled at him. "Don't worry, Cor, I don't think Madame LeFabre will have time to skate with us if she's going out to lunch."

The ice was a grey reflection of the sky above them, the trees which sheltered the lake were wind-still. It was indeed ideal for skating. Georgina kneeling to fasten their skates, glanced around her. It was much warmer—the ice looked the same and Julius had said that they could skate. All the same, she circled slowly round the lake before going back for Beatrix.

It was on their second time round, when they were exactly opposite Cor, watching them from the further bank, that the ice cracked suddenly beneath their feet, and Georgina, making a frantic effort to save Beatrix, pitched forward into the ever-widening gap in the ice.

Mercifully, she had Beatrix by the hand; she clutched it still as she fought her way to the surface. As soon as they came above water, she gasped:

"Don't scream, darling. Keep your mouth shut, and stay still. When I tell you, get an arm around my neck."

She began to tread water, a difficult, almost impossible feat because of her skates; but she was a good swimmer and not given to panic.

In a moment, she said, "Now, darling," and felt a small sodden arm weighing her shoulders. She could see Cor now, staring at them in a kind of stiff horror which permitted of no sound. She drew a deep breath and called desperately, "Cor, listen carefully. Go slowly—slowly, you hear—to the drive; it's very close, then shout for help."

She spluttered on a mouthful of icy water and heard his faint cry and hoped he had understood, and still treading water, watched him turn and make his way carefully along the little path, out of sight, towards the drive, that was, thank heaven, so close.

Beatrix had begun to cry, had swallowed water, and was choking. Georgina hushed her with chattering teeth, drew a difficult breath, and essayed a shout. It wasn't very successful, but at least it gave them both the feeling that help would come quickly. Beatrix whimpered, "I can't feel my legs." She had gone very white, and her arm was like lead.

Georgina shouted again; her voice sounded thin and useless in the still air; her legs were getting numb too, she could feel their heavy, slow movements. She tried to remember how long it was possible to keep alive in freezing water—five minutes—ten? She judged that four or five minutes had passed already, although it was hard to tell. She said:

"Darling, can you try and get your other arm around my neck?" and Beatrix had just managed to do that when she heard a car's engine in the distance. Cor would be on the drive by now; even if the car went by, someone in the house would be sure to hear him. The car snarled into the drive and she heard its grinding halt, presumably by Cor. Before her terrified senses could think who it was, Julius's voice came to them from the bank. He said with an icy calm, "Keep still. When I reach you, do exactly as I say."

She said nothing, because her teeth were clenched to stop their chattering, but she gave a weak squeeze of the limp little body she was clutching so desperately. It was only seconds later when he was beside them, pulling Beatrix's arms from her neck. He said, "Hold on!" and was gone with the little girl over one great shoulder. The seconds seemed like eternity; it was lonely in the water; she heard shouting and running feet, but they didn't mean anything any more. She closed her eyes, went under, and came up again, gasping and choking and terrified, to find Julius there. He had a rope this time; he put an arm around her and clamped her close while they were pulled to the bank, where several pairs of hands caught her and laid her flat and began to rub life back into her body.

Her teeth were rattling in her head, but she managed, "Beatrix?" and for a moment Hans' nice elderly face loomed above her. He said, "O.K." and smiled encouragingly. She remembered something else. "Cor?"

"Also O.K."

"Open your mouth," said the Professor in a voice she didn't care to disregard. She dragged her teeth apart and spluttered and coughed as he poured brandy down her throat. She opened her eyes then, and stared up into his face. It was white and looked somehow bony. His eyes were blazing with rage which he made no attempt to conceal. She closed her eyes again and whispered, "I'm sorry...." and heard him say in a voice as cold as the ice itself, "You fool—you little fool! You might have drowned!"

She felt the tears creep into her eyes and thought that probably the brandy was making her maudlin. He was rubbing her arms with steady strength, seemingly unworried by his own soaking clothes. She would have liked to explain how it all happened, but when she opened her eyes again it was to encounter his bleak look, so she said instead:

"I'm all right now. Shouldn't you go to Beatrix?"

His eyes darted blue fire so that she shut her own against them.

"Hold your tongue," he said in the same icy voice. "Beatrix is in good hands," and he picked her up and carried her as though she were a bundle of feathers into the house, and up the stairs and into her room, where someone had spread a blanket on the bed. He dumped her on to it without ceremony and said harshly, "Get undressed and have a hot bath. I'll send Pankie up," and went away without so much as a glance.

It was wonderful what a hot bath and a brisk rub down did. She washed her hair and dressed again, then piled her hair neatly again and did her face, and leaving Pankie to clear up the mess, went in search of Beatrix.

She was sitting up in bed, looking almost normal, but when she saw Georgina she burst into tears, and said, "George, dear George! I thought we were going to die, didn't you? I was so frightened." She held out her arms and Georgina said in a soft motherly voice, "Oh, darling, I was frightened too, but you see Julius came and rescued us, didn't he? Only I'm so sorry, poppet—it was all my fault...."

Dimphena, walking in with a tray, heard her. "Your fault?" she cried indignantly. "How could it be? Beatrix said that Therese Le Fabre told you. . . ."

Georgina's white cheeks went a little whiter. "It was a mistake—I'm sure she made a mistake—Julius isn't to know. You won't say anything, will you—promise?"

"Why?" asked Dimphena stubbornly. "Why should you take the blame?"

"I'll explain later, only don't say anything."

Two pairs of blue eyes gazed at her. "If you say so," said Dimphena, "we promise."

Georgina got up. "Thank you. I must find Cor—is he downstairs?"

Dimphena nodded. "Julius was looking at his legs." She saw Georgina's face. "They're all right," she added hastily.

"He didn't tell Julius?"

187

"I don't think so, because Julius took him to the kitchen to Hans, because he said he had to telephone somewhere or other and tell Therese to come back here."

Georgina looked puzzled. "But she said she would probably go skating. She must have left the house soon after us. . . . I'll find Cor."

He was sitting in one of the Windsor chairs drawn up to the scrubbed table in the middle of the vast kitchen. He was drinking milk, and lifted a milky moustached mouth from his mug as she went in.

He said instantly, "Dear George. I was brave, wasn't I?"

He smiled seraphically. Now that the fright was over, he was enjoying the important part he had played in the adventure.

She went and sat down beside him. "Very brave, Cor. I can never thank you enough—you saved our lives because you did as you were told. You're a knight in shining armour."

He beamed anew. "Yes, I am, aren't I? I'd do anything for you, George—and Beatrix," he added as an afterthought.

It was her chance. "Would you really, my dear? Then promise me something. If Julius asks you what happened, don't tell him about the message Madame LeFabre gave us—to tell you the truth," she went on untruthfully, "I think there was a muddle and I'd rather explain to him myself."

He looked doubtful. "Is Cousin Julius cross with you?" He drew miniature brows together. "If he is, I don't think I will promise."

She said hastily, "No, no. Why should he be cross?"

He finished his milk. "All right, I won't say anything."

"Dear boy!" She got up, and he asked, "Where are you going?"

"Well, I'm a bit cold and tired and I don't want any lunch. I thought I'd go to bed—just for an hour or two, you know. Dimphena said she'd look after you. Do you mind?"

188

He shook his head. "Is Beatrix going to stay in bed too?"

She nodded. "She got awfully wet and cold, but if she stays in bed today, she'll be as right as rain in the morning."

"You too?" he asked anxiously.

"Me too," she said.

It was lonely in her room. Hans came with a tray of coffee and soup, but she had no appetite. She said rather timidly, "Do you think I could stay here? Would anyone mind—could you possibly say that I'm asleep if—anyone asks?"

He smiled so kindly at her that she turned her back so that he should not see her trying not to cry, and he said to her from the door:

"Leave it to me, Miss Rodman. You shall not be worried, I promise."

The day passed slowly. Pankie came in without speaking and made up the fire, and Hans came about four o'clock with some tea, and presently Dimphena, with the news that the children were fine, and that Therese had come back long after lunch, and was even now in the study with Julius. Georgina shivered, and Dimphena said quickly, "George, you've caught cold— for heaven's sake get into bed." She got up. "I'm going so that you can undress now."

It seemed a good idea. Georgina trailed around the room, taking down her hair once more, and washing off her carefully applied make-up. When she was finally ready, she decided to go and see Beatrix for just a moment, to make sure that she was quite recovered. She opened her door quietly and started along the corridor. She had taken perhaps ten paces when she heard Julius's voice from the hall. He spoke clearly and quite slowly to some unseen listener below her, and what he said rooted her slippered feet to the spot.

"I was mad to invite her here. I do not wish to see her again, though I suppose I am bound to meet her at some time in the future."

There was a feminine murmur in reply, but she didn't wait to hear more. She went blindly back to her room, and got into bed, and lay shivering from a coldness that had nothing to do with her tumble into the lake. Somebody came in later—Pankie, to make up the fire, but she pretended sleep, and presently, she actually did sleep. The heavy, deep sleep of exhaustion. She still slept when the Professor came in and stood by the bed, looking down at her. He pulled up a chair and sat patiently for a long time, and when she didn't stir went away again.

She awoke early, unrefreshed, bathed and then, still in her gown, fetched her case and started to pack. Probably Julius wouldn't want to see her again, but he would have made arrangements for her to go—she might as well be ready. She was half done when there was a knock on the door. She glanced at the clock on her bedtable; it was still very early; barely seven. Perhaps Pankie had been told to call her. But it was Julius who came in. He shut the door behind him and leaned against it, slowly observing the heap of clothes on the bed beside the open case, and then her tear-stained face. He looked at her for a long time, tender and amused and mocking. Presently he walked over to the bed and tipped everything out of the case and closed it.

"Pankie will put everything away for you later," he said pleasantly.

She was staring at him, the tears still running down her cheeks from eyes round with surprise. She wiped them away impatiently with a very damp handkerchief, sniffed and said, "But I'm going away. I meant to pack yesterday, but I went to sleep. . . . I—I heard you in the hall—I don't eavesdrop," she added with dignity, "but I couldn't help it—you were talking so loudly, and I was on the landing."

He was sitting on the edge of the bed, watching her. "What was it I said?" he asked, still very pleasant.

"That you had been mad to invite me here and that you didn't wish to see me again, though you supposed you would be bound to some time in the future. Though I can't see why, because you never came to Casualty before Cor and Beatrix had their accident."

She had spoken in a hopeless little voice choked with tears. Now she blew her poor red nose once again and said, "Do go away," and then, quite crossly, "Go away!"

He got up from the bed and walked over to her, took her handkerchief from her and threw it down and gave her his own. His arms felt warm and loving, and quite unnerved, she cried dolefully, "You were so angry."

"Darling heart, men are always angry when they are frightened—and I have never been so frightened in my life before as I was when I saw you in the lake."

She said in a whisper, "But you don't want to see me again. . . ."

"Dearest, if you had come downstairs, you would have seen that I was talking to Phena, and I could have told you that Therese had already gone."

"Gone? But how did you find out?"

"Well, you know, Cor is no fool even though he's only seven. He promised not to tell me, but he made no promise that he shouldn't tell Hans. When Therese came back, I—er—asked her what had happened. She had, I believe, intended it as a kind of joke. At least that is what she said."

He pulled her closer. "Dearest Georgina, I love you; from the moment I first saw you in Casualty, I loved you."

"Then why did you call me Miss Rodman and Nurse and make me wear a uniform?" She was a little peevish now, knowing she looked a fright with her hair streaming untidily down her back, and a tear-streaked face. He said, reading her thoughts as he so often did, "I couldn't wait any longer, my darling. I came to see you last evening, but you slept so deeply—I wanted to tell you that it was you I loved, and not Therese; that she didn't matter and never had mattered. I was going to tell you that I asked her here because I was angry with you for preferring a Sister's post to marrying me."

She looked at him with some indignation. "But you didn't ask me. . . ."

He kissed her again in a wholly satisfactory and masterful fashion.

"I wanted to ask you when we first met, but I had to be fair; I had to give you a chance to see what life with me would be like. You had to decide for yourself if you could be happy, with two homes in two countries and a ready-made family of four children, as well as children of our own. I imagined it might be easier for us both if I treated you as a nurse and not as the girl I wanted to marry. I do not know about you, but for me it made no difference at all."

Georgina lifted her head from its comfortable position against his shoulder. "Are you going to propose to me now?" she wanted to know. "It's not very glamorous. . . ."

He laughed. "Dear darling, do you want soft lights and roses and sweet music? You shall have them all, I promise you, but now I cannot wait any longer. Will you marry me, Georgina?"

She said yes.